33 Baggott's Circle

Lisa Ashby

Based on true events

Second Edition

For Jason,

who has supported me in everything I do

Prologue

In the heart of England, on the outer edge of the county of the West Midlands, the small ex-mining town of Shrewhill was basking in the afternoon sun. Blackbirds and sparrows chirped and tweeted as they collected sticks to build nests in the newly sprouting trees, but their songs were easily drowned out by the steady flow of traffic that constantly filled the roads around the outskirts of the town. On one such road, a young lady of medium height and slender build was running as though the devil himself was chasing her.

The lady's long dark hair trailing behind her as she ran down the Coventry Road, which seemed to get longer with each stride. By the time she'd rounded the corner onto School Lane she was out of breath, drenched in sweat and her heart felt like it would explode.

At the top of School Lane the lady had to stop and wait for a car to pass before she could cross Charles Avenue and cut through the church yard. She bent at the waist and took several deep satisfying breaths and as soon as the car had passed her by she straightened and ran across the road into the small cemetery that encircled St. James' church.

The church grounds were full of ancient trees that soared into the sky, their branches spreading out to shade the area and provide temporary relief from the unseasonally warm sun. Beams of sunlight cut through the canopy and glinted off the long strands of webbing from countless spiders that made the place their home. The lady dashing through the area would normally marvel at the sight but she was supposed to be meeting her mother after work and she was very late.

She rounded the church and headed down Kilner Street and turned right onto High Street. Millie sped past the butcher's shop and waved to Terry through the window, he waved a pork chop back at her then hastily dropped it on the scales. Millie caught sight of her mother sitting at the bus stop talking to Mrs Taylor who still lived next door to the house where Millie had grown up.

As soon as she reached the two ladies, Millie said a breathless "hello" to Mrs Taylor and a hasty "sorry I'm late" to her mother.

"I thought you weren't coming," Ruby complained as she looked at her daughter. She stood up and stepped on the cigarette she had just dropped. "See you soon Betty," Ruby said as she patted Mrs Taylor's hand. The old lady said goodbye and the pair walked away.

It was a strained hour long shopping trip, with not much conversation between the ladies. Ruby was still put out that Millie had kept her waiting and Millie was tired from working, running and dealing with her mother's sullen mood. As they were walking up Churchill Road towards Millie's home they passed the local council office. Millie looked at the 'For Rent' notice board, as she always did, and saw that 33 Baggott's Circle was finally available. It had been empty for a while, the council usually have a quick turn over of their housing stock, but for some reason, 33 had taken months to get ready.

"Come on Mother!" she said and she grabbed Ruby's hand and marched through the office door. Ruby didn't have time to say "I'll wait here", in less than two seconds she found herself in the office and Millie was asking to see Rob Mickelwright, the manager. The young lady at the desk seemed a little out of sorts with Millie's brisk attitude but before she could reply Rob's voice boomed across the office, "come on Millie, I'm not busy". Ruby sat in the waiting area with the shopping and Millie marched over to Rob's office. He was sorting through a stack of papers in the centre of his desk, which he moved to the side so he could wave Millie into the only other chair in the cramped room.

She hadn't even reached the chair when she said "I want to apply for 33 Baggott's Circle. I see it's finally on the list."

"What no foreplay? No 'hello darling, how are you?' Straight to business, as usual."

"Cheeky sod! Hello Robert, how are you on this fine afternoon?" Just as Rob inhaled to answer, Millie cut him off "I want to apply for 33 Baggott's Circle. I see it's finally on the list!"

He started to laugh but a speck of spit went down the wrong way, the sound came out as a bark, splutter, giggle and cough all mangled into one bizarre racket. In the entrance hall, Ruby and the pretty young thing behind the desk heard the noise and looked at each other. In the office Millie sat innocently and patiently waited as Rob finally stopped barking, wiped his eyes. "I'm sorry Millie, there's a family with four kids who need it more than you and they're due to move in next Wednesday. I wish I could help but you have a home, these guys don't," he said.

Millie sank a little lower in the chair but suddenly sat up straight. "A family of six? You haven't forgotten that we live in a four bedroom house? 33 is only a three bed, they can't move there. It makes far more sense if they take our house, which has four huge bedrooms, and we take 33 which is more suited to our needs."

Rob sat forward and rested his elbows on the table. He chewed his bottom lip for a few seconds and mulled over what she had proposed. "You know, that's not a half bad idea." He saw Millie smile and his own lips curved a little. "Don't get your hopes up yet. I'll get in touch with the family and put the idea to them. If they agree to the change I'll have one of the girls call you and arrange a viewing. If they don't want 41, I'll call you myself and give you the bad news."

Later that day, Millie sat with her husband Joe and asked for his thoughts on moving there, but he hated the idea. Joe had never liked the upheaval of moving, he disliked any change of routine, plus his parents had lived in this house for over twenty years and he didn't want to let go of their last home. But after Millie had told him how unhappy she was here and that there was a family in need of their large home, he relented.

Early the next morning just before Millie was due to leave for work, the phone rang. "Hello, this is Tracey from Shrewhill Neighbourhood Office, can I speak with Mrs Holden please?" a high pitched female voice asked.

"Speaking," Millie replied.

"Oh hello, Mrs Holden, Mr Mickelwright asked me to call you to arrange a viewing of 33..." the lady paused and Millie heard the shuffling of papers down the line "...Baggott's Circle. Would tomorrow at 4pm be convenient?"

Millie clutched the receiver a little harder, her heart was pounding and her hands started sweating. "That would be perfect. Thank you. We'll be there!" After she put the phone down she let out a squeal of excitement, grabbed her handbag and ran out the door to work.

By the time Thursday afternoon arrived, Millie was a bag of nerves; she couldn't wait to get her hands on those keys. It was approaching 4.15 and they were still waiting to be shown around the house. Joe checked his watch again and grumbled: "if they aren't here soon, I'm going back home."

Millie swore under her breath then turned to him. "Go home if you want, but for God's sake stop moaning!"

A few seconds later a silver car turned the corner of the street, pulled down the straight road which formed into a large circle where the street got its name. 33, a semi detached adjoining number 31, sat at the middle of the circle and faced towards the opening of the street. The car pulled to a halt and as soon as the engine stopped Rob Mickelwright got out and greeted the family. He ducked back in the car to get a clipboard, his muffled voice drifted out to them. "Sorry for keeping you all waiting, spot of bother at the office."

He closed the door and walked up to the house and swiftly opened it and walked in. None of them were aware of the curtains twitching in the upstairs window of the adjoining house.

Millie and Joe were more than happy with the house: the walls were all clean; there was still carpeting down in the two larger bedrooms and living room, and all three looked immaculate; the upstairs bathroom was smaller than the one they had now, but it was newly tiled and the airing cupboard in there had a fresh coat of paint on.

While Millie and Joe were content with everything they had seen, their six year old daughter Leah was happy enough in the garden and downstairs, but became distressed when they walked into what would be her bedroom. Looking at the room with massive brown eyes, she hugged herself and in a tiny voice she said: "I don't like it, the room's breathing mummy". Millie laughed and said she was imagining it.

Joe looked around and almost immediately saw what he thought the problem was. He walked over to the window which had been left slightly open and with a swift yank he pulled it shut. "It was the wind coming in!" he said and pointed to the wall beside the window. "Look here, the wind was getting behind the wall paper; it just looks like the room is breathing." Leah seemed happy enough with that explanation and after a little giggle at her own silliness; she did a twirl and skipped from the room.

Millie looked at Joe to get his approval, which he gave with a short nod of his head. She kissed him and went back down stairs to speak with Rob with Leah happily trailing behind her. Joe, alone in the room, felt a brief chill and the hairs stood up on his neck. In the distance a child giggled. He rubbed his arms and made his way back down the stairs.

When Joe entered the living room he saw Millie signing the papers Rob had brought along. "Ahh, Mr Holden if you could sign here, I'll give you the keys and leave you to it." Millie passed him the pen and he added his name to the paperwork. "Welcome to your new home!" Rob looked at the both and sighed, "now the bad news. The Jones family will be moving into 41 next Wednesday so that only gives you until Monday to vacate and get the keys to us." With that said, he muttered a quick "goodbye" and left them to get on with the job of moving.

1

Saturday April 25th 1981

Millie stood by the back window and watched Joe dismantle the old wooden shed. What time was it? She yawned briefly, wiped the spots of moisture from her hyacinth blue eyes and looked at her watch. It was 1.13pm. They had been up since 5am to get ready for the move to the new house and it was nearly done. The large four bedroom house in Baggott's Circle was almost empty and it had only taken just over a day to sort, box and almost clear.

Granted there was still a little work to do, but when Millie had put the word out among her friends in the street that she and her family were moving and they only had the weekend to do it, they dropped everything to help. An army of her neighbours, organised by her good friends Joan and Linda, marched into the house carrying boxes and took over the whole operation. The men carried the furniture, which the ladies had stripped of their ornaments and cleaned. All that was left to move were two bookcases, a single bed belonging to her daughter Leah, the bed she shared with Joe, the three piece suite and a mountain of boxes stacked in the living room.

She turned from the window and wiped an errant strand of hair from her forehead. There was a bowl of soapy water on the floor beside her, into which she dipped a cloth ready to wipe down the first bookcase. Her mind wandered to what had brought her to this house.

Millie had met Joseph Holden in 1964 when they were both nineteen and working at a factory called Oaken Hayes, where 90% of the population of the town had worked at one time or another. Millie had just started working there as a cleaner with one of her duties being to take tea to the staff on the production line where Joe had been working.

Millie had been instantly attracted to the handsome man with large doe eyes the colour of chocolate and thick brown hair slicked back in the '50's style. Each day she brought drinks for the workers she would linger and chat with him and while Millie was vivacious and outgoing, Joe was painfully shy. After a few months of waiting for Joe to invite her out but him never quite getting around to it, Millie had taken the bull by the horns and asked Joe if he would like to go to the cinema with her, to which he agreed. In less than two years they were married and as they couldn't afford to rent their own place, they began life together living with Millie's parents.

Millie was bought out of her daydreaming by Joan, who had just walked into the living room carrying two steaming mugs of tea and had an old tea towel draped over her arm. "There ya go our wench," Joan said as she passed a mug to Millie, "get that down you."

"Thanks Joan, I'm parched." Millie dropped her cloth into the bowl at her feet and eagerly grabbed the mug. "I can't believe how quick we got this place cleared. I can't thank you all enough."

"Don't worry about it pet. We're happy to help." Joan took a sip of tea, placed her mug on the fire place and started to dry the bookcase Millie had just finished washing.

Millie took a sip of tea and sighed. "I'll miss having you next door."

Joan laughed, "ya daft sod you're not moving to Timbuktu! Besides, Linda lives next door so you can share gossip over her fence instead of mine."

"Ha, true," Millie said and smiled at her friend. "It's a lovely house and it would be perfect if it wasn't for Jellyman living next door." She gave a mock shudder and made an "eughh" sound.

"Yeah, but you don't have to share a path with him, he lives the other side so you probably won't even see him."

Just then the front door opened and in rushed Joan's son Bill and his brothers Matt and Stewart.

"Mrs Holden, we can't get any more stuff in the little bedroom, we'll have to put these in the living room," Bill said as he waved his hand in the general direction of the 'box mountain'.

"Cheers Bill, there's not much more to move, just what's left in here."

***

7.50pm

It was almost dark out now. Joe was checking the upstairs to see if they had remembered everything and saying a silent 'goodbye' to all the memories he had of this place. The arguments with his sister Doris in her bedroom, all the nights he'd sat looking at the stars in his room and the day he'd heard his mother screaming after finding his father dead in their room. So many memories, some were incredibly sad but most were good and wholesome, and Joe didn't want to leave but he understood Millie's reasons for needing a change of scenery.

Downstairs in the kitchen Millie could hear Joe walking through each room shutting the doors as he went. They had been married almost fifteen years and she still felt like a school girl when she looked at him, but as much as she loved him Millie had never felt such overwhelming love as when her daughter was born in December 1974.

By the time Leah had come along both she and Joe had moved twice: first in 1967 to a small flat in a newly built block called Talbot House and in 1970 they moved in with Joe's mother, Alice. Joe's father, Eddie, passed away suddenly from a massive stroke and Alice found living by herself in the big house too much to cope with. She was a proud woman but she was also lonely and out of desperation she all but begged the couple to move in with her. Millie hadn't wanted to leave her lovely little flat, but she saw the merits of moving in with her mother in law: a lovely big house with a long garden, great for growing their own fruit and vegetables, and they would be able to save money by just paying board instead of all the bills.

Alice was a short, small framed woman with wispy white hair which she always wore in a bun at the nape of her

14

neck. She was well liked in the street and was the one everyone asked for in an emergency. Alice would tend the sick, comfort the bereaved and had, on occasion, laid people out when they had passed away.

While she was an angel to her neighbours, Alice could be a demon to live with. She knew she needed help with the house, but she acted as though she resented Millie's presence in it. The house was depressingly dark and had all the warmth of a tomb and Millie wanted to paint the walls to brighten the place up, but Alice flat out refused. Millie wanted to try and make the place feel more like her own by rearranging the furniture and using pieces belonging to her and Joe that were in storage, but Alice wouldn't hear a word spoken about it.

There were constant spats between the two ladies until one day in mid '74 when Millie shouted: "if I lose this baby because of the stress you're causing, I'll never forgive you!" Alice's attitude changed dramatically when she found out Millie was expecting and while the house never got redecorated and the furniture remained unmoved, life was easier in 41 Baggott's Circle.

Alice passed away two years ago and in an effort to make the house finally her own, Millie spent hours with Joe's help decorating and finally replacing the old fashioned furniture with their own. But no matter what she did, she could still feel Alice's presence and that did not sit comfortably with Millie. She knew she would only find peace by moving to a new home.

2

Saturday April 25th 1981
8.15pm

Linda Pember lived at 35 Baggott's Circle with her husband
Phil and daughter Jayne. She had lived there all her life
having been born in the house on Christmas Day 1945. She
was a small woman with a mass of curly dark hair and
permanent smile that lit up every room she entered. At
present the smile had gone to be replaced by a look of
determination as she tugged at a dandelion that had just
started to emerge in her flower beds under the living room
window.

Hearing foot steps behind her, Linda gave up on the
weed and turned to see Millie and Joe walking towards their
new house, instantly the smile was back in place.

"Hello my loves," Linda greeted them both with a
hug. "The beds are set up and made. There are clean towels
in the bathroom and everything else you might need in the
bathroom: toothbrushes, soap and the like."

"Thanks Lin," Millie said. Leah came bounding out of
Linda's house just as Millie spoke and ran straight to her
mum. "Did you thank Auntie Lin for looking after you?"

"Thank you for letting me stay and play with Jayne
and thank you for the sandwich." Leah said shyly, her voice
barely above a whisper.

Linda bent down so she was at Leah's eye level.
"You're welcome," she whispered back. She straightened
and said: "we'll keep Moses a few more days until you're a
bit more settled. He's been a bit cranky being in a strange
house, but he's eating OK." Moses was a short haired male
cat, two years old with black fur and pea green eyes. He had
been the runt of a very large litter and was tiny in
comparison to the other kittens, but he had been the only
one to investigate the humans who were looking for a new
companion. Joe and Millie instantly fell in love with the tiny

ball of fluff and decided then and there that he was going home with them.

Jayne poked her blonde head out the door and yelled: "hello Mr Holden. Hello Mrs Holden, can Leah play here tomorrow?"

Millie smiled and replied that she could and soon after they parted ways. Joe opened the front door and let Millie and Leah walk in first, then he swiftly followed. The stairs to the first floor were directly behind the front door. The door to the left opened into the living room which was haphazardly arranged with furniture and a new 'box mountain'.

Leah yawned and rubbed her eyes. "Tired matey?" asked Millie. Leah was going to reply but as soon as she opened her mouth, another huge yawn escaped. "Right, bed for you miss."

"I'll take her," said Joe as he swiftly scooped up his daughter. Holding her weight easily on his arm, he marched up the stairs and turned left onto the landing. The first door that met them was to the bathroom, which was a fairly small room that somehow held a bath, sink, toilet and an airing cupboard, the door of which was slightly ajar. A large towel was draped over the side of the bath and a new bar of soap lay on the sink next to a glass containing three toothbrushes.

Joe stepped into the bathroom and pushed the airing cupboard door shut and turned the latch. "Right Shortie, brush your teeth and go to the loo and don't forget to flush! I'll get your bed ready." Joe set her down by the bath and went to go through the next door along the landing, which was Leah's new room.

Linda had made the beds earlier so that was one job they wouldn't have to worry about. Joe had just turned down the blankets on the single bed when he heard Leah call out: "Daddy, I can't find the toothbrushes!"

***

When Joe got back down stairs he found Millie frantically searching through some of the boxes in the living room. As soon as she rummaged through one she was on to the next, the room was a mess to begin with but now it looked as if a bomb had hit it.

"Mill, what's wrong?"

"My pills! I can't find any of them." She closed another box and set on to the next. "I thought I'd marked the box, but I can't find it anywhere." Millie was near to tears. She had been diagnosed with high blood pressure back in '74 when she was carrying Leah. The doctor was convinced it was to do with the pregnancy but after Leah was born, it refused to go down and steadily increased over the years. She was on a combination of blood pressure tablets and, more recently Frusemide as she had been having issues with water retention.

"Do you need them tonight?" Joe asked as he helped her look, but he already knew the answer.

"No, you know I take them in the morning. But I want them handy for when I get up." Millie was frustrated and her sharp tone indicated that.

"Mill. Leave it tonight, we'll get up early and look again in the morning. They'll turn up." She dropped the lid of the box back down and sighed. "OK, I'm sorry I snapped. I'm mad with myself for not keeping them in my bag. Why did I have to pack them in a sodding box?"

Joe turned away and walked into the kitchen, "I'll put the kettle on." Thankfully, someone had the foresight to plug in the fridge and hook up the gas stove.

Two hours later, the living room was starting to look more organised. 'Box Mountain' was now more of a hill which resided under the large east facing window; the bare bookcases were along the wall opposite the window, which separated this room from the kitchen. On the wall adjoining Mr Jellyman's house was a chimney breast with a tiled mantle and gas fire at its centre, and two deep alcoves on either side: one by the window where a chair now lived and the other on the kitchen side where the Philips TV had been set up. Joe had been kneeling in front of the thing for the last thirty minutes trying to tune in BBC1, BBC2 and ITV, but he couldn't find a signal for any of them. The large sofa was positioned in the middle of the floor and was currently filled with towels, some of the family's clothes and curtains.

"That's it! I can't keep my eyes open any more." Millie stretched and winced as her back cramped from bending over so long.

"Still can't get a signal with this bloody thing!" Joe yanked the aerial out the back of the TV and stood up.

"Let's worry about it tomorrow, I'm off to bed. Are you coming?" Millie grabbed an armful of towels and yawned as she walked to the stairs.

"I'll make sure the doors are locked, be up in a bit."

Millie turned on the landing light and trudged up the stairs to the bathroom. She turned on the bathroom light and noticed the airing cupboard door was open; she dropped the towels in there, swiftly pushed the door shut and turned the latch. The light bulb flickered as she washed her face and dried it on the towel which was balled up and lying in the centre of the bath. Hearing Joe walk upstairs, she finished her ablutions and left the room, but no one was there. "Millie, you're losing it," she mused as she walked passed Leah's room to the next door which was the master bedroom. The room was situated over the living room and had the same shape, including the chimney breast and a large east facing window, through which the moon shone bright illuminating the room with the help of the two street lamps in the centre of the circle.

On the wall which adjoined Leah's room was the bed that had been made earlier, but it was rumpled as though someone had been bouncing in the centre of it. She straightened the blankets and quickly changed into her nightdress then crawled into bed on the side by the door. A few minutes later Joe came in and got in the other side of the bed. They cuddled for a few moments and it wasn't long before they began to drift to sleep.

***

Millie woke with a jolt, her heart was racing and sweat covered her body. The room was quiet except for the occasional snuffle from Joe as he slept. She had no idea what had woken her, some noise maybe or the sense that she was being watched? She looked out onto the landing but couldn't make out anything, the moon and street lights were still illuminating the bedroom, but the light didn't reach beyond the open door way.

Her heart was still thudding in her chest, but she couldn't settle. Slowly, so she wouldn't disturb Joe, she crawled out of bed and tiptoed to the door. She held her breath and inched her head around the side of the door frame and peeked into the hallway, first towards the smallest bedroom to her right, then she turned and glanced towards the bathroom. The door was wide open and something was lying on the floor. She looked back to see if Joe was awake, but he was still bundled in the blankets and breathing deeply. She stepped out into the hall and began to creep past Leah's room, whose door was still shut. As she got nearer to the bathroom, Millie could see that the odd shape on the floor was the towel that she had found balled up in the centre of the bath, which she had left folded ready for Joe to use.

Two more steps brought her to the bathroom door; she braced herself for the blinding light as she pulled the light cord. The light came on and with a loud creak the airing cupboard door flew open with such force it hit the wall. "SHIT!" Millie yelled. Her heart felt like it was in her throat and it took her what felt like five minutes, but was more like five seconds, to take a breath. "Stupid fucking door!"

"Mummy, you said a bad word." Millie jumped as Leah's little voice called to her, her hand clamped to her chest as she spun round and saw her daughter standing in the doorway. With a nervous laugh Millie sagged against the wall, "yes! Yes, I did. I'm sorry, I said a bad word." She straightened and pulled the light cord. "Now let's both get back to bed." Grabbing Leah's hand Millie walked purposefully from the bathroom.

3

Sunday April 26th 1981
7.30am

"Morning Mrs!" Joe smiled as Millie sat on the side of the bed, she turned and he noticed the dark circles under her eyes.

"Didn't you sleep last night?" He reached out and stroked her back as he spoke.

"I did, but I heard a noise and went to check it and that stupid airing cupboard door opened and scared me half to death. I couldn't get back to sleep after." Millie got up and changed her clothes. Joe lay there admiring her slender frame as she stripped off her nightdress and threw on a skirt and blouse.

"I locked that yesterday, twice. The latch must be faulty. I'll have a look later."

"OK. Our Frank's bringing mother over this afternoon. She's going to help me sort the kitchen out. See you downstairs." She smiled tiredly and left the room. Joe lay back and listened as her steps walked along the landing and receded down the stairs. His eyes closed for a few moments, but opened swiftly as Millie shouted his name.

He jumped out the bed and bounded down the stairs. Millie was standing by the mantle; she turned as he entered the living room. "Look!" She pointed to the mantle and there were her pills, all laid out in a neat little row, in the order that she took them each morning. "How the hell did they get there?"

"I haven't the faintest idea." Joe walked over and stood beside Millie, "it wasn't me."

"Well it couldn't have been Leah and I definitely didn't do it. I couldn't even find the bloody box they were in." Millie grabbed the pill boxes and went to the kitchen leaving a bemused Joe standing in the living room.

***

21

"Where do you want these?" Ruby was standing by the sink drying the plates she had just washed, a cigarette hanging from her mouth which dropped ash as she spoke.

"Mother, please put that out. I'll have them here." Millie grabbed the clean plates and put them in the cupboard by the living room door. Ruby took a long drag on her cigarette and threw it into the fire place.

She was a slim woman and had been stunningly beautiful in her younger years with her bluebell tinted eyes and thick auburn hair. Even now as she approached her sixtieth birthday she was still attractive although her eyes had lost some of their lustre and her hair was now white apart from a permanent yellow nicotine stain at the front. She was always smartly dressed and refused to go outside the house without her hair covered with a headscarf.

Ruby had been happily married for thirty-five years to Bill Norton who she had met just after the war ended in '45. He was a strapping fellow of almost six feet, with dark curly hair, eyes the colour of cornflowers and a chest you could get lost in. She idolised him and missed him every day since his untimely passing in May 1978. She was more fortunate than some of her widowed friends as they lived alone, whereas she shared her home with her son Frank who was the living image of his father. And while she never really had a loving relationship with her daughter, she was more than happy to look after Leah and took every opportunity to spend time with her.

Ruby wiped her nose on the back of her hand and looked out the kitchen window to the back yard, which was covered in grass and weeds. The right side of the garden butted against the Pember's garden and was divided by a nearly new four foot high fence. However, the left side against Mr Jellyman's garden had a hedge row of Leylandii trees which had to be at least ten feet tall. "That needs trimming."

"What?" Millie was putting cans in the cupboard in the little pantry to the side of the sink and couldn't quite hear what Ruby had said.

"That bloody monstrosity out there," she gesticulated to the hedge, "it needs to go!"

"I quite like it and at least we won't have to see that weirdo next door" came the reply.

"Suit yourself, but I think it looks a mess."

"Maybe you're right," Millie emerged from the pantry and stood to look through the window. "It is a bit messy, but we've more than enough to keep us occupied right now. The hedge can wait."

Ruby looked at Millie. "Have you eaten today?"

Millie shrugged, "we had some toast this morning. We've been too busy to think about food."

"Well that's easily sorted." Ruby dropped the tea towel on the sink and marched into the living room to Frank was crouched in from of the TV tuning in the last channel. She emerged a few seconds later, "I've sent Frank to the chippie. Do you have any bread left?" Millie pointed to the counter. Ruby grabbed the margarine out of the fridge and began to spread it on the remainder of the bread.

***

Frank was upstairs helping Joe arrange the furniture in Leah's bedroom, they had just finished eating and he'd downed a can of beer to wash the taste of grease away. He picked up the bedside table and let out a monstrous belch. "Get out and walk you bugger!" he said. "Where do you want this Our Kid?"

Joe pointed to the alcove on the left side of the chimney breast. Leah's room followed the same pattern as the master bedroom. Both rooms had originally had a cast iron fire place to keep them warm, but some time over the last forty years, they have been removed and the holes bricked up. But Leah's room was above the kitchen, the only room to still have a coal fire, so all year round it would be warm. Even though the windows were open, it was stuffy in the room and both men were sweating.

"If we put that there, her bed can go next to it along here." Joe drew a rectangle in the air in front of the chimney, "and the wardrobe can go in the other alcove there."

"Right you are." Frank put the bed side table where Joe pointed. Joe shoved the bed into place then went over to the other side of the room to help Frank move the wardrobe to where he wanted it.

Millie came in with a washing basket full of Leah's clothes and a pair of old blue fibreglass curtains with a gaudy brown and orange flower print. She was looking for a place to put the basket when she noticed that the wallpaper was peeling on the wall behind the bedroom door. She dropped the basket and tugged the paper. With barely no effort at all, the whole section of paper came away from the wall.

Millie looked in horror at the sight that greeted her eyes. "Oh god! Joe, look at this." Joe turned and couldn't believe what he was seeing. The wall had pentagrams carved into it which had been filled in with white plaster of Paris so that they stood prominently.

"No wonder the paper wasn't sticking down properly!" Joe said to no one in particular as he examined the markings. The white plaster was uneven and it was plainly obvious that not enough paste had been used to hang the paper.

"I don't want Leah seeing this. Do we have any paste?"

"No, I'll have to get some when I finish work. We'll have to move the wardrobe back for now and do it tomorrow before she gets in from school." Joe looked at Frank, "will your Ma be OK with picking her up from school and keeping her until we get this sorted out?"

"I don't see why not. She can come over tonight if she wants, saves you having to worry about hiding it."

Joe and Millie both agreed and that night Leah slept on her Nan's sofa.

When she returned home the next day the wallpaper was back in place, she was completely unaware that anything was amiss.

4
Saturday May 9th 1981
10am

Leah was sitting on the floor in the living room eating cereal and watching cartoons. She finished and took her bowl into the kitchen and asked her Mum if she could go upstairs to play.

Millie was standing by the fireplace brushing her hair ready to go out. She had a thick head of dark hair which was almost long enough to sit on. On warm days like today, she often thought about cutting it off as it could be unbearable, but she could never go through with it.

"Don't you want to go shopping with me?" Leah shook her head and said she wanted to play in her room. "OK then but if you're going upstairs, don't pester your dad, he's working on the landing."

"OK mummy." Leah hugged her Mum and ran upstairs.

A flock of pigeons flew past the windows. Millie groaned as she could hear Jellyman outside calling his birds home. In the eleven years she had lived in this street she could count on one hand all the times she seen Mr Jellyman. When she did see him, Millie would deliberately walk across the street to avoid crossing paths with him: not because she was afraid of him, but he absolutely reeked of pigeons and the smell could knock you back. He was an old, short fat man with a widow's stoop and stains on his clothes that didn't bear too much scrutiny. His eyes were small and dark and he wore a constant sneer on his bloated face. Millie dreaded the thought of having to speak to him, but she knew that eventually she would have to; she didn't want those horrid things shitting on her washing.

Millie finished getting ready, grabbed her handbag and shouted a quick goodbye to Joe and Leah.

Joe was getting ready to start hanging wallpaper at the top of the landing. He had spent the morning washing

25

the walls ready for the woodchip paper to go up that could be painted in the evenings after he and Millie finished work.

He wasn't looking forward to getting this job done, the landing had a massive drop over the bottom of the stairs and he wasn't all that great with heights. The small bedroom at the front of the house ran over the stairs, so there was a section of wall with nothing but a sheer drop under it, but Joe figured he could reach that by leaning over the banister on the landing. The most difficult part would be doing the long section of wall that ran down from the loft all the way to the stairs. It was at least twelve feet from top to bottom, for that he would need to brace the ladder against the bedroom wall and one of the stairs. Joe decided to do that part first to get it out the way. He was just about to set up the ladder when Leah came out of her room, where she had been quietly playing with her doll for the last hour.

"Can I go downstairs and watch TV?"

"Go on then, but don't have it too loud. I'll be on the stairs so you won't be able to come back up." Joe tugged on her ear as she walked past him, making her squeal.

"Yes daddy," she called as she made her way downstairs one step at a time.

When Leah was out of the way, Joe braced the ladder against one of the middle steps and propped the top against the little bedroom wall opposite. He picked up his tape measure and climbed the ladder which was surprisingly sturdy. He extended the tape measure and took a rough measurement of the wall and added an extra foot just to be sure he'd have enough paper. Joe had already set up a bucket of paste and a table just inside his bedroom which he used to measure, cut and paste the first piece of paper.

He stuck a cloth in his back pocket and folded the paper, paste sides together, and climbed back up the ladder. He placed the paper so it just over lapped the ceiling and butted up against the corner of the overhang. He smoothed down the first few inches to make sure it adhered, then slowly opened the other folds and let the paper hang limply against the wall. Joe started to smooth the paper at the top and noticed how taught it had suddenly become was as though someone was holding it straight down. Happy his daughter was helping him, Joe said: "that's right Leah, hold the paper there and …"

Joe looked down and he nearly fell off the ladder. He swallowed hard, not quite believing his eyes, but unmistakably the paper was being held some six inches from the wall, but no one was there. He blinked several times and still the unseen hands held the paper away from the wall as though waiting for him to finish smoothing it out. Joe wiped his forehead with the cloth and in a somewhat strained voice said: "thank you, I can manage now." No sooner had he finished speaking, the paper fell to hang against the wall. A split second later a scraping sound above Joe's head caught his attention and looking up he noticed the attic cover had been moved out of position.

***

When Millie got in from her shopping trip she found Joe sitting in the kitchen, Moses lay on his lap purring as Joe absent-mindedly scratched his ear. Joe was still mulling over his earlier experience and didn't hear the door open, he almost jumped out of his skin when Moses meowed and dropped to the floor.

As soon as she had finished putting the groceries away, Millie poured them both a cup of tea, then sat opposite Joe and asked him what was troubling him. In calm measured tones he told her what had happened that morning. Millie had always been a believer in spiritual phenomena and after finding her pills laid out for her their first morning here, she had no reason to doubt his story.

"Are you OK?" Millie asked him.

"Yes, yes I'm fine now," he reassured her and put his mug on the table. He started to laugh, "I wasn't earlier. I nearly fell off the bloody ladder. I got most of it done, just the wall with our bedroom doors on to go, but I'll do that tomorrow." He stood up and went to the back door, "right now I want to have a good look round the back yard, see what needs doing. Love you."

"Love you too." Millie replied, her face lit up with a dazzling smile.

Joe walked around the back of the house and took stock of the messy yard. The first section was constructed of poured concrete which was cracked in several places, but was still fairly even. This ran from the overgrown hedge on the left the tall section of wooden fencing on the right and stretched out some eight feet from the house. The rest of the garden was a jungle, overgrown with grass, weeds and what looked like medieval burial mound at the bottom of the garden in the left corner. Joe picked his way across the garden to get a better look.

There was a tall fence along the bottom of the garden that separated the gardens of Baggott's Circle from those in Mill Place. Along the left side of fencing, behind the mound, were three large conifer trees which had all lost their bottom branches, those that remained were overgrown and completely blocked the light. The whole area behind the mound had a grotto feel and if he were a kid again, Joe knew he would spend all his free time here.

Joe turned and studied the Leylandii's, which were also severely overgrown and needed at least four feet taking off the top. He made his mind up to make a start on that tomorrow afternoon after he had finished papering the landing. He started to walk back down the garden and had almost reached the concrete when he saw the net curtain in Leah's bedroom window had been pulled to the side. Joe stopped and watched as a Leah's little face looked out of the window, he smiled and waved. She moved closer to the window, smiled and waved back.

Joe frowned and lowered his arm. It must have been a trick of the light but it looked for all the world like Leah was deathly pale and frightfully thin. Just then, the sun peeked out from behind an errant cloud and the light blinded him. Joe raised his hands again but this time to shield his eyes. When he looked back to the window Leah had gone and the curtain hung in its usual place.

5

Monday July 6th 1981
7.30am

Millie was dressed and ready for work. She walked down the stairs and grabbed her handbag from one of the hooks behind the front door. She also took her coat, though she was sure she wouldn't need it as it was already warm outside.

Joe was in the front room getting Leah ready for school. "Do you need your P.E kit today?"

Leah was sitting on the sofa brushing her doll's long black hair, "not today. Can I take Julie with me?" she asked as she proudly held up the doll, its nylon hair still in knots and the red dress it wore bunched up around its tiny waist.

"No," Millie told her on her way into the kitchen.

"But mummy, everyone takes their toys in."

"I'm sure they aren't supposed to, but in any case your mum said no, so that's that." Joe said as he finished tying Leah's shoes. She stuck out her bottom lip and pouted.

Millie dropped her bag and coat on the table and went to the mirror above the fire place and reached to grab her hair brush from the mantle. Lying beside it was a letter addressed to her mother, she could tell by the writing it was from her Uncle Norm who still lived in Martley in Worcestershire where he and Ruby had both been born and raised. When World War Two broke out, Ruby decided to move to Birmingham and found work in the laundry of the local hospital. Ruby had wanted Norman to join her, but he was engaged to a local girl and so he decided to stay in the small village.

"Mother must have brought it and forgot to tell me," Millie said to herself. She picked up the envelope and saw it was open, so she took it out to read...

'Hallo Ruby,

29

How are you my dear? I was so happy to hear Millie and the family had got themselves a nice new home, pity it wasn't closer to you. Susan and I are planning a small trip to Wales in the next couple of weeks so if you call and we don't answer, don't worry. We would both love for you to come for a visit when we get back, if Frankie can bring you to ours, we will bring you back and we can visit Millie and see the new house.

We have some exciting news ourselves! Brenda is expecting, you know how long she has been trying for a baby. We're over the moon! I can't believe we will finally be grandparents. As soon as we return from our trip I will call you, your number is still the same isn't it?

Can you send me Millie's address please? Send our love to Frank, Millie and the rest of the family.

We love you and can't wait to see you,

Love,
Norm and Susan'

Millie folded the letter, put it back in the envelope and placed it back on the shelf, then made short work of brushing her hair and tying it back in her usual style. She quickly boiled water for a cup of tea and shoved bread under the grill for some toast.

Half an hour later a knock sounded on the back door knocked and opened to reveal Ruby's smiling face. "Hello chick," she said to Millie who was almost ready to leave.

"Hello mother. Leah's just getting her coat on."

"Nanny!" Leah came bounding into the kitchen. Moses hissed and ran into the living room.

Ruby bent down and kissed her cheek, "are you ready for school?" Leah nodded and complained: "Mummy won't let me take Julie to school." Ruby looked up at Millie and mouthed, "who?"

"Her doll," Millie mouthed back. Ruby rolled her eyes and looked down. "Well, you wouldn't want to lose her would you?"

Leah answered swiftly, "no nanny, but I don't want to leave her here in case the ghost scares her!"

"I'm sure she'll be fine if you leave her here. Uncle Frank is outside in the car. Do you want to wait for me there?"

"OK." Leah ran to Millie and kissed her. "Bye mummy. Bye daddy," she shouted before bounding out the back door, school bag in hand.

Ruby opened her handbag and started to rummage through it. "What's this about a ghost?" Millie spent the next few minutes telling her about the incident with her pills and what happened to Joe a couple of weeks previously and a few other odd incidents like the attic hatch always being open, the airing cupboard that refused to stay shut, personal possessions disappearing and reappearing and more recently hearing walking in the bedrooms when no one was upstairs.

"There's no such thing as ghosts, you're making it up!" Ruby snapped as she carried on searching through her bag. "Blast it! I must have left it at home."

"What are you on about?" Millie asked, slightly irritated.

"I've had a letter from your Uncle Norm and I've left it at home."

"You mean this letter?" Millie walked over to the fire place and took the envelope off the shelf and handed it to Ruby.

"How in God's name did you get it?"

"You must have bought it with you last time you came over."

"I did not! I only got the bloody thing this morning!" Ruby grabbed the letter and shoved it deep into her bag. She straightened her headscarf and tucked in the errant white hairs at the side of her face in an effort to try and regain her composure. "You best be going, you'll be late for

31

work! Say 'hello' to Joe for me. See you later chick!" She gave Millie a peck on the cheek and hurriedly left the house.

Joe came into the kitchen a few seconds later with Leah's doll. "Has Leah gone? I wanted to show her I got the hair straight." He shrugged and threw the doll on the kitchen table and left to get his shoes on for work. Millie giggled as the doll landed on its back with its legs akimbo and bright red dress hitched up around her waist.

"Come here you little floozy!" Millie picked the doll up, closed its legs and pulled her dress back into place. "There, now you're much more respectable." She smoothed the hair back down and set her back on the table.

***

Leah was in the playground of the Burford Infants and Junior school that she attended with Jayne Pember. Both girls were in Class 2 and were always getting in trouble for talking during lessons. During free time, they were usually seen standing or sitting heads together deep in conversation about something or other. Anyone seeing them together would instantly recognise the pair as they were as different as night and day. Leah had brown eyes and chestnut brown hair that her mother always tied into a ponytail, with a fringe that completely covered her forehead. Jayne, in contrast, had bright blue eyes and short blonde hair that glittered in the sunlight. Where Leah was shy and spoke softly, Jayne was boisterous and always talked with a loud voice.

"Did you bring Julie?"

Leah pouted. "No, mummy wouldn't let me."

"You should have just put her in your bag, she wouldn't know. I brought Marie with me, look she has a new dress!" Jayne dug her hand in her bag and pulled out her doll, who was wearing a new ball gown with dainty little sequins around the bottom of the skirt.

"Oh, that's pretty! Mummy is going to make Julie a new dress soon. Oh no, my nose is running." Leah opened her bag to find the handkerchief Millie always threw in there "just in case". She let out a little squeal of surprise, "Julie's in here, daddy must have put her in there for me so mummy wouldn't find out." She hastily wiped her nose on her coat sleeve and grabbed the doll to show to her friend, but was rudely interrupted by the school bell.

The bell had just been rung to signal to the children that they must stand in their class groups ready to go to their respective rooms and begin the school day. Each class group had a designated spot on the playground where the children had to stand in line. Leah and Jayne ran to join their line, but made sure they were at the back so they could put their dolls back in their bag without being seen by the teachers.

A hush fell on the rows of children as the headmaster, Mr Humphries, came out and walked slowly down the path to stand in front of them. He was a tall man and could see every face staring back at him as well as those two at the back who were clearly not paying attention. Leah was standing just in front of Jayne in the line so she had to turn away to finish what she was doing, but this gave the casual observer the impression that she was ignoring the headmaster.

Recognising the culprit Mr Humphries called out: "Leah Holden stay behind." A few giggles could be heard as he spoke, but a sharp look from Mr Humphries soon silenced them, "the rest of you may go into school." The children began to walk away one class at a time starting with the youngest. Leah felt Jayne pat her back as she walked past.

Leah stood there with her eyes wide open as Mr Humphries came to stand in front of her. "So young lady, do you think it is acceptable to talk when I am talking?"

"No Sir," she whispered.

"And what, may I ask was so important that it could not wait until break time?"

"I was showing my friend my doll and I was putting her away when you came out. I..." Leah's voice trailed off as she finally found the courage to look at the man in front of her.

"I see. I shall look after her for you." He held out his hand and waited for Leah to reluctantly place the doll there. "You may have it back at the end of the day. I shall be calling your mother and reminding her that toys are not permitted at school. Now you may go to class."

***

"Could Millie Holden report to the office? Phone call for Millie Holden in the office." Millie was on her break in the canteen when she heard the announcement on the overhead speaker. Her stomach dropped, no one rang her while she was at work unless it was an emergency.

"Would you clear that up for me June?" she asked as she shoved her cup towards the lady at her table.

"Of course, I hope everything's OK!" came the reply, but Millie barely heard as she started to run to the administration office.

As soon as she reached the door, she knocked and went straight in. Marge was manning the phones today and she was already taking another call.

"Hold the line please. Line two Millie."

Mille thanked her and picked up the second phone on Marge's desk, pressed '2' and greeted the person on the other end of the line.

"Mrs Holden, this is Mr Humphries. I'm calling to inform you that Leah has been reprimanded for bringing toys into school."

"I'm sorry, I did tell her this morning that she could not take toys in."

"Be that as it may, her doll is sitting on my desk. I have asked Leah to collect it from my office this afternoon and I have informed her that I would contact you about the incident."

"Her doll? The one with the black hair and red dress?" Millie was confused, it couldn't possibly be that doll, she had placed it back on the kitchen table before she and Joe had left the house.

"That's the one." He let out an exasperated sigh and continued, "I've not punished Leah, she is after all a good pupil and has never caused an issue before, but I shall have to offer some form of punishment should there be a recurrence."

Marge had finished her phone call and watched as Millie said "I understand, goodbye!" and dropped the receiver back into its cradle. She was still deep in thought when Marge asked: "Everything alright Mill?"

"What? Oh yes, nothing major, the headmaster at Leah's school just calling to let me know she's in trouble and 'would I kindly have words with her when I get home?'" she said in a fairly passable imitation of Mr Humphries' gravelly voice.

Marge chuckled, "that's OK then, when I took the call I was worried she was ill or something."

Millie smiled and thanked Marge for taking the call. She spent the remainder of her shift wondering how that bloody doll had jumped off the table and into Leah's hands at school. It just wasn't possible.

6

Friday July 10th 1981
4pm

Over the weeks since the family had moved in the house had been transformed almost beyond recognition. The living room, hallway and landing had been painted with a soft cream emulsion and the wooden skirting boards and doors were freshly painted with a light brown gloss which complimented the walls. The kitchen was a soft sky blue as was the bathroom. The bedrooms had yet to be papered but the walls were clean so there was little urgency to decorate those rooms.

The garden had also been worked on. The shed from the old house had been rebuilt and a stack of wood lay in a pile by the hedge ready for Joe to start work on building a new one. The leylandii trees were trimmed back so they formed a tidy flat wall along the length of the garden and Joe had even managed to cut four and a half feet from their height without Jellyman next door raising so much as an eyebrow. The grass had also been cut back and Millie had dug the ground nearest to the house for a vegetable patch. Strawberries, runner beans, lettuce and potatoes were planted and growing nicely.

Leah and Jayne were happily playing in the back garden of Leah's house, as they had been doing every evening after school since Leah had moved into 33. They had invented a fabulous new game which involved the mound at the bottom of the garden and a huge piece of cardboard that Jayne had brought over one day. Taking it in turns, one girl would sit on the cardboard or 'the slider' as they called it, while the other would drag it down the mound. After a few rounds the girls would lie on the side of the mound to get their breath back and see what shapes they could see in the clouds. When they were rested, the game would begin again leading to more squeals of laughter.

It had been five days since the doll incident and Leah still could not believe that she had not got into trouble. She had sat through the remainder of her lessons biting her nails and imaging all sorts of punishment from her mum. But when Millie had walked through the back door after finishing work, she just smiled at Leah and said she had brought fish and chips home for dinner. To Leah, it was as if the whole thing had never happened apart from a brief "please don't take your toys to school", nothing more was said on the matter.

She didn't know that her parents had spoken in depth about the doll and the other strange things that had occurred since moving into the house. After their talk, they both agreed that Leah should not be told if anything 'bizarre' happened, she was only six and they didn't want her scared of being in the house.

"That's a dog." Leah pointed at a huge fluffy cloud.

"And I see a fish," Jayne squinted and pointed to the sky.

"Oh yes! One more go on the slider?" Leah laughed and sat up. Jayne followed and grabbed the cardboard. Leah sat on the slider and Jayne gave a tug and pulled Leah down the mound. Leah's stomach flipped as she slid down the mound making her squeal with laughter.

"My turn!" Jayne shouted and the slider was reset. Jayne sat on the board and burst in to giggles as Leah pulled the slider and tripped and fell on her bottom. Both girls lay in a heap laughing at what had just happened.

"SHUT THE FUCK UP! EVERY FUCKING DAY IT'S THE SAME! GET IN THE BASTARD HOUSE!" Jellyman's voice boomed from the other side of the hedge.

The girls screamed and scrambled to their feet. They took off running back to Leah's house and hid behind the wall and listened as the old man next door continued his rant about "those noisy bastard brats upsetting his birds!"

Millie had not long arrived home from work and was washing her hands at the kitchen sink. She had been taking more time than usual as she was watching the girls play and reminiscing about her own childhood. She had just begun to dry her hands when she heard the racket from next door; she dropped the towel and ran to the back door when the girls bolted towards the house.

Leah and Jayne were standing by the back wall of the house, peering around the corner at the hedge. Both were shaking and had their hands to their mouth.

"Girls, what did he say to you?" Millie asked. She crouched down and hugged them both. Leah began to cry when she saw her mum, which angered Millie: not that she was angry at Leah, but that the old bastard next door thought he had a right to shout at her child.

"Mrs Holden, he shouted a bad word and told us to stop making so much noise."

"Did he now? Jayne you should go home and tell your mum."

"Yes Mrs Holden." Jayne hugged Leah and ran through the gate to her own back yard, yelling for her mum all the way.

Millie wiped Leah's face and kissed her forehead. "Go in the house and wash your face my love, I won't be long."

Leah started to ask where she was going, but Millie shushed her and gave her a gentle push towards the kitchen then watched to make sure Leah went in and closed the door behind her.

Millie could still hear Jellyman rattling around his garden muttering to himself as he went. She rounded the corner of the house just as a flock of fifty pigeons flew over her garden, just clearing the top of the hedge.

"Are you still there you mad old bastard?" Millie shouted as she got by hedge.

"WHAT?" Jellyman yelled back.

Millie gingerly climbed on Joe's wood pile which was a good two feet high, it wasn't perfect but it was solid enough to hold her modest weight. Luckily the hedge thinned in this one spot, so she reached up and parted the branches to look down at the old man. What she saw disgusted her and made her retch.

Jellyman was standing with a limp pigeon in his hand, its bloodied head hung from its body and swayed slightly. Blood and feathers were splattered on one corner of the shed where he had just bashed the bird's brains in. Millie watched as Jellyman hobbled over to the bin he kept by the hedge and she nearly vomited when he lifted the lid. Hundreds of flies erupted from the bin and a putrid smell hit her, she closed her eyes but not quick enough to miss the sight of the rotting corpses of several cats and pigeons stowed inside.

Jellyman looked up and saw her watching him. He nonchalantly threw the poor dead bird with the other unfortunate animals and dropped the lid back on the bin. Flies still buzzed around him, which he seemed not to notice at all. He wiped his hands on his already dirty shirt.

"What do you want?"

"Just to give you fair warning you disgusting pig! Do not ever shout at my child again or I will not be responsible for my actions."

"Tell that noisy shit to keep out the back yard in future. Her and that friend of hers are always making a racket and upsetting my birds!"

Millie stood on her toes so she could look more imposing. "I shall do no such thing. She has every right to play in her own back garden. You raise your voice to her again and I'll swing for you. Now get back to murdering your flying rats you filthy old bastard!" With that she let the gap in the hedge close and dropped down off the wood pile.

7
Saturday July 11th 1981
12pm

The day was slightly overcast and thunderstorms had been predicted. Millie was outside pegging the laundry on the line and with every item she hung, she would look at the sky and pray the rain would hold off until it was all dry. She finished that task and went back into the kitchen to begin emptying the twin tub washing machine. The pump wasn't working as it should and she had to tilt the machine on its side to get the last of the soapy water to drain away. She had often thought of getting an automatic, but this old thing still cleaned the laundry perfectly, so she plodded on week after week and put up with its quirks.

"Can I play outside today mummy?" Leah had been watching TV, but she wanted to go out and play on the slider with Jayne.

"Yes, but please, try to keep the noise down." Millie looked down at Leah who was smiling brightly as she honestly thought her days of playing outside were finished. Millie smiled back at her and leaned down to kiss the top of her head. "Go on then and if it starts to rain come in straight away!"

"Yes mummy!" Leah said as she ran out the back door. Millie could hear her yelling for Jayne to come and play and in less than thirty seconds the two girls were racing down the garden.

The girls were breathless by the time they reached the mound, the cardboard slider was still propped against it where they had left it yesterday, having forgotten it in their eagerness to escape from Mr Jellyman.

Leah was the first to reach the mound and she dropped on to the slider to catch her breath. As the sun broke out from behind a cloud something glinted on the grass beside her. She reached out and picked it up; it was the shattered bottom of a glass bottle. Jayne had been busy picking daisies with the intention of making a daisy chain. With her hands full of the tiny flowers she dropped to the mound and screamed in pain as her knees hit the soft grass.

Leah frantically jumped up and asked Jayne what was wrong. Jayne was crying hysterically and shouting for her mother. Leah ran as fast as she could to the house and almost collided with Millie who was running to see what the commotion was. In no time at all Millie reached Jayne who was desperately trying to stand but could not manage it. Millie knelt beside Jayne and gently turned her over to see what was causing her pain. As Jayne rolled to the side Millie could see blood pouring down the girl's leg and an ugly piece of glass embedded in her knee. Millie wasted no time and carefully scooped Jayne up in her arms and carried her next door to her parents.

***

"And she's alright now? ... Did she have stitches? ... Oh the poor love ... I'm so sorry this has happened Lin ... I know, but I feel responsible ... Not yet, but I have a fair idea though ... OK, thanks for letting us know ... Send Jayne our love ... Bye." Millie replaced the receiver and looked at Joe who was staring at the mound through the kitchen window. He drained his mug and set it in the sink. Beside him on the draining board sat a bowl half filled with broken bottles. As soon as Millie had come back from the Pember's house and told him what had happened, he went straight to the mound and discovered at least forty jagged pieces of glass, all perfectly positioned with their sharpest points facing upwards. "They say she's alright, thankfully there was no dirt in the wound. Poor thing had ten stitches."

"How the hell did it get covered in glass in the first place?"

"It can only have been that mad bastard next door. He wanted me to stop the girls playing in the yard and I said I wouldn't." Millie came up behind Joe and wrapped her arms around his waist. "I feel so responsible. Oh Joe..." her voice broke.

41

He could feel her body shaking, "hey, don't cry love." Joe turned and wrapped his arms around her and held her as she cried out her frustration. "It's not your fault. You didn't put that glass there."

"No, but I shouted at him. I got him mad enough to do that." She pulled away from him and waved her arms. "I bought us here!"

"Millie, you're upset and you've every right to be, but you are not to blame. You didn't make that man a monster; he did that all by himself. I admit, moving here was your idea, but we would not be here now if I had put my foot down and said "no", so I share some of that responsibility."

"But..."

Joe silenced her with a kiss. Millie sighed and wrapped her arms around his neck and held on as the kiss became more passionate. Slowly, reluctantly, he pulled away and dropped a brief kiss on her forehead. "Care to pick this up later?" he whispered.

Millie giggled and looked at him from under her lashes, "I could be persuaded!" She squealed as Joe swatted her behind. Millie laughed as the stress of the last few hours slowly began to ebb away.

"You feeling better love?" Joe asked as he stroked her cheek. She nodded and was about to reach up for another kiss when a crack of thunder boomed across the sky loud enough to make the whole house shake. Moments later huge drops of rain splashed against the window.

"No! My bloody washing!" Millie and Joe both dashed outside and headed for the washing line to gather the clothes which were almost as wet as when Millie first pegged them out.

***

It was just approaching 6.15pm when Joe thrust his fork into the ground and hit something solid, the impact sending shockwaves up his right arm. The storm that had passed over earlier in the day was very brief and was in fact just the edge of a larger cell which quickly drifted east towards Lichfield. Joe's dad would often say: "if a storm heads towards Lichfield it'll be back later." Joe never knew whether to believe that or not, but always humoured the old man when he said it. As soon as the rain cleared Millie pegged out the washing for the second time that day and Joe began to dig away at the mound.

He cleared the grass from the top and laid it to the side ready to put back in place after he had levelled the ground. He knew it would take a lot of effort on his part, the thing was monstrous. It stretched almost ten feet from the overgrown hedge and was at least eight feet across. Its sides sloped sharply to a height of four feet and had a several divots in that the girls had used as steps to reach the top. There was a lot of soil to move and Joe had spent the better part of three hours digging and had just barely scratched the surface.

He dropped the fork and shook his arm to try and relieve the throbbing in his elbow. When the pain subsided, he picked up his fork and slowly pushed it into the soil six inches to the left of the solid strike. The fork easily slipped into the soil then stopped as it hit something equally as solid as before. This happened a further eight times as Joe tested the ground in a circular pattern radiating out from the original spot.

"How's it going love?" Millie called as she walked up the garden with Leah trailing behind, who was sad that she wouldn't be able to play on the slider anymore.

"It was going fine until just recently. I hit something and I have no idea what the hell it is. I'll start early tomorrow and see what's down there." Joe gathered his tools and joined Millie and Leah as they walked back to the house. Thunder rumbled in the distance as the three made their way through the back door.

8

A crowd of people were gathered in the garden of 33. As soon as the news spread of the discovery, they wanted to see it for themselves, including Mr Hodgkins, who lived at number 7, a house on the straight section at the top of Baggott's Circle.

Old Man Hodgkins, as his neighbours affectionately called him, was one of the first people to move into street when it was newly built in 1937, along with his wife Mary and six month old son Archie. Back then he had been a strapping man of thirty-two, with thick muscles honed from his years down the local mine and a mass of carrot coloured hair. Age and frailty had stripped the muscles from his body and the colour from his hair, but his wits were as sharp as a tack and when Old Man Hodgkins heard about the car buried at the bottom of the Holden's garden he had to take a look.

Joe had been up since 8am and after having a hasty mug of tea, he had set to work to find out what was under the dirt. As the hours went by and the dirt was removed, the internal components of a 1930's style motor car were slowly becoming visible. First the seats, their leather rotted away to show their internal springs, next the dashboard and steering, then the gear lever, handbrake and headlamps. All that seemed to be missing were the engine and the body of the car.

While Joe continued to dig, a steady stream of residents meandered in and out of 33's garden to take a look at the strange discovery. He was just about to stop for lunch when he saw Old Man Hodgkins leaning over the side of the pit on gripping Archie's arm for support. Joe was about to greet both of them when the old man started to crow with laughter. "So the silly old fool did bury it after all!"

"Sorry Mr Hodgkins? Do you know who did this?" Joe squinted against the brightness of the sun as he spoke.

"Eh? Oh yes, the old guy who lived here. Savage his name was, he was as daft as a cart load of monkeys." The old man laughed again.

Joe stood and stretched his back; he was aching from being hunched over most of the day. Joe looked back at the pit and said "so this was his car. Why did he bury it though?"

Mr Hodgkins laughed again. "The silly old fool went to war in 1940, before they started building Mill Place over there," he pointed towards the estate behind Joe's garden with a gnarled hand. "Back then there was a dirt track there and you could get to the Burntwood Road from this garden. So he parked it here and left thinking he could drive it again when he got home. Boy did he have a shock!" He broke into another peel of laughter. "Thirty new houses across the back of his garden and no way to get it out! Well, he couldn't plough through the new estate and there weren't enough room between the houses to drive it into the Circle. He reckoned that he'd sold the body for scrap, and sold the engine and wheels to the bloke across the road, then buried what was left of the bugger!"

"I see it, but I still can't quite believe it!" Joe shook his head a smile breaking out on his face.

"Neither did I until now. Oh is that your little girl up there." Mr Hodgkins lifted his hand and waved to the child he had seen in the upstairs window. "She doesn't look too well, is she alright?"

Joe looked up and saw the emaciated face of a child staring out of Leah's bedroom window.

***

"So let's make a list. Thank you dear!" Martha Brookes took the paper and pen Millie handed her and began making notes.

Millie H. - sandwiches: cheese, egg, ham

Joan C. - fairy cakes, fruit cakes (no candied peel)
Linda P. - salad, cheese and pineapple, sausage rolls
Tracey J. - trifle, jelly (orange and strawberry)

Anne Haywood intervened: "I'll bring cocktail sausages and make vol-au-vants as well."

Martha looked slightly irritated but smiled sweetly and added that to the list. "So that just leaves drinks for the adults, fizzy pop for the kids, paper plates, plastic cutlery and cups."

"We could have a couple of raffles to raise the money for those." Millie suggested.

"Excellent idea, we could all donate a prize each and sell tickets around the street. We'll ask for donations towards the food while we're at it." Martha looked among the group to gauge their reaction. Nobody outright agreed with her, but nobody dissented either, so she was happy with that.

Millie's living room was packed with ladies from around the circle: Kathy Gough from 19; Meg Willis from 23; Martha from number 25; Anne Haywood from 27; Joan from 43; Linda from next door and Tracey Jones, who lived with her husband and children in Millie and Joe's old house. The Royal Wedding was fast approaching and after the success of the Queen's Silver Jubilee celebrations in '77, the organisers of that event wanted to do something to celebrate Charles and Lady Di getting married.

"We have a large tent which we could put in our front yard for all the food. We'll use our sound system so we can have a bit of a dance later on." Martha looked around at this last suggestion and saw nodding heads, so she smiled and finished by saying. "There's just over two weeks to go 'til the big day ladies, let's do our street proud."

When she finished speaking she stood and the ladies took that as their cue to leave. Millie went to the front door and waved them all goodbye, just Joan and Linda stayed in Millie's front room. Millie was about to shut the front door as Tracey Jones hesitated, turned and came back down the path.

"Mrs Holden can I have a quick word?"

"Of course, what can I do for you?" Millie smiled at the young girl.

"I just wanted to thank you for what you did for us. We were going to move here if you recall, but you are a wise lady and I can't thank you enough."

Millie shrugged, "it just seemed the right thing to do. You needed that big house, we didn't."

"We love it there and we're so happy. I hope you're as happy in your new home." With that, she turned and walked down the path, stopping just long enough to wave back at Millie.

Millie waved back and went back into Joan and Linda.

"Wow, I forgot how bossy Martha can be." Joan stretched in the big chair and put her hands behind her head.

"You're not wrong! 'We can use our tent and our sound system!'" Linda said in a high pitched voice.

Millie laughed as she sat in her usual place on the sofa and curled her legs underneath her. "What a bizarre couple of days it's been." She reached out and patted Linda's arm. "How's Jayne?"

"She's fine. Her leg is sore, but she's happy enough now she has a new dolly to play with and a mountain of chocolate from her dad. He spoils her, but I can't blame him after yesterday."

"Lin..."

"I know what you're going to say and you can stop right there Miriam Holden. It was not your fault!" No one ever called Millie by her full name, apart from her mum and dad when she was in deep trouble. Throughout her life she had always been Millie, or Mill to her nearest and dearest, everyone knew not to call her Miriam.

"Yes Mum, I'm sorry!"

"Cheeky sod!" Linda laughed and stood to leave.

Joan looked at the clock. "Bloody hell, it's nearly eight! I best get back." She got out of the chair and walked with Linda to the front door. Millie uncurled herself from the sofa and followed so she could lock the door behind them. They hadn't quite reached the living room door when Joan said: "I'll nip back after school tomorrow so I can have a look at that car."

"OK Joan, but our Frank is coming by to help us take it to the tip so you better be quick."

"Right you are pet. Bloody hell!" Joan shouted as she watched a small vase slide along the bookshelf. The colour drained from her face and she blinked several times trying to make sense of what she'd just seen.

"What's up Joan?" Linda asked, her back was to the room so she missed it completely.

Joan swallowed and pointed to the vase which by that time had stopped moving. She leaned on a sideboard Millie had recently bought and started to chuckle. "My old eyes must be tired I swear I saw that sodding vase move!" She picked her hand up and pointed to the vase in question and the thing immediately shot off the bookshelf and landed on the floor with a thud.

"That's it, I'm off! See you Mill!" And with that she beat a hasty retreat.

"Millie, what's going on with this house?" Linda asked, concern and shock at what she had just witnessed clearly visible on her usually smiling face.

Millie sighed and bent to pick up the vase which miraculously hadn't broken in the fall. "I have no idea Lin. Things move, the airing cupboard door keeps opening and closing, the attic hatch refuses to stay down and we hear banging on the walls. Oh yeah and Joe swears someone was helping him hang wallpaper when we first moved in. What with him next door as well as all this, I'm beginning to regret moving here!"

9
Wednesday July 29th 1981
The Royal Wedding

It was a gloriously sunny day, warm with a slight breeze; it was perfect for a street party. The ladies in the unofficial organising committee had done an excellent job with the preparations. Over the last two weeks, several raffles had been held amongst the residents of the street, the proceeds from which were enough to buy the food, drink and a huge haul of paper plates, cutlery and plastic glasses.

The tent had been erected in the Brookes' front garden and their stereo blasted out a mix of 60's and 70's music. Millie had made yards and yards of red, white and blue bunting, which now adorned the tent where the food was laid out.

Everyone had stayed home to watch the wedding on their TVs then as soon as the bride and groom came out on to the balcony of Buckingham Palace and kissed, the TV's were turned off, the food brought out and the party started.

The ladies of the street were huddled in groups talking about how beautiful Lady Di looked and wasn't her dress magnificent with its long train? The men were in groups drinking beer and talking about the football season which was due to start in a few weeks and wasn't the price of tickets a rip off these days?

The kids all ran about laughing, dancing and eating the fairy cakes that Mrs Caldwell had made and trifle the nice lady from 41 had brought over. They weren't really bothered by the wedding, they just wanted to eat and play with their friends.

Millie and Joan were standing in the circle watching some of the kids playing. "Are you ever going to come to ours again?" Millie asked.

"Maybe in a few years, when I'm too old and decrepit to care about the ghost." Joan laughed. "Seriously, how can you live there with all that going on around you?"

Millie shrugged. "You get used to it after a bit."

Joan rolled her eyes and started to walk towards the food tent, "I need a sandwich and a huge drink! Want anything Mill?"

"No thanks." She looked about her and saw that Leah was dancing with a group of her friends and Joe was chatting to Jerry Brookes, Martha's husband and Phil from next door, no doubt telling them about the buried car. It had taken over a week for Joe to dig the rest of the car out of the ground and several trips to the scrap yard to off load all the bits and pieces he had found. But the thing was finally gone, the hole was back filled and the grass re-laid.

Leah and Jayne continued to play out on the back garden and were out there nearly all day now as they had broken up for the six weeks holiday, ready to start in Class 3 when they returned in September. Surprisingly, there had been no more trouble from Jellyman; in fact he had been rather quiet lately. Although they still heard him calling his birds in, there had been no more instances of him shouting at the girls.

Leah came running over to Millie and asked to use the toilet. Millie needed to go herself so she walked with her to their house. Millie unlocked the back door and walked into the kitchen. "Go on, you go first. Don't forget to wash your hands!"

"OK mummy!" Leah called as she climbed the stairs.

Moses ran to her and purred as he wrapped himself around her legs. She bent down and stroked his ear making him purr even louder. With a soft thud, he rolled to his back and wriggled his exposed belly for Millie to scratch it, she duly obliged. Moses stopped purring and abruptly turned his head. His eyes dilated and he rolled onto all fours and growled. Millie stroked his back as he hissed at something unseen and bolted to cower under the kitchen table.

Leah was sitting on the toilet behind the bathroom door. She finished and got up and crossed the short distance to the sink where she washed her hands and dried them on the towel draped over the side of the bath.

Suddenly she felt uneasy in the little room and a creaking noise behind her made her jump and spin around. The cupboard door was open wide and in the dark recess two red glowing eyes peered back at her. Leah stood rooted to the spot and stared, she opened her mouth to call for her mother but no sound came out. The red eyes blinked and a hiss emanated from the dark recesses of the cupboard. Leah let out a huge scream and bolted from the room.

Millie was just coming up the stairs and had made it halfway when she heard Leah's ear piercing scream. She bounded up the last few steps and met Leah as she left the bathroom.

"Baby, what's wrong?" Millie dropped to her knees and held Leah.

Leah couldn't talk. Great sobs wracked her little body. "Mummy..." she gasped for air, "there was..." She took another gulp of air, "a monster... in there..." She couldn't finish. She clung to Millie as another wave of tears and wailing came over her.

"Shush, it's OK. Nothing can hurt you. Are you sure you saw a monster?" Millie felt Leah's head nod against her neck. "Let's take a look, come on."

"Noooo!" Leah clung harder.

"OK, shhhh. Go to your room and wait for me there, I won't be long." Millie wiped the tears from Leah's face then got up and went to the bathroom leaving the door open so Leah could come in if she felt brave enough. The cupboard door was still wide open and the towel Leah had used was in a heap on the floor. Millie closed the door with a shove and locked it again. Joe had replaced the old catch, but still the door was often found open. Maybe they should nail the stupid thing shut!

Leah was lying on her bed talking softly to Julie when she heard the toilet flush. A few moments later, saw her mother smiling at her by her open bedroom door. Millie held out a hand, "it's gone, so you needn't worry. I think your scream frightened it away." Leah let out a breath and ran to her mother and followed her downstairs.

"I know you said you saw something but I think you're tired and had too much sun. That can make you think you saw things that aren't really there." Millie really was clutching at straws with that one. She truly believed Leah had seen something but she was desperate to explain away what had just happened so Leah wouldn't be scared.

"Do you really think so mummy?" Leah frowned and thought for a second and decided that her mother may have been right; it was after all a very hot sunny day.

Millie looked for Moses as they walked back through the kitchen and saw he was drinking from his water dish. Millie locked the door behind them and they went back to the party.

Moses took a few more laps of water then jumped up on the kitchen table where he sat licking his paws and cleaning his face. He was chewing a knot out of his fur when a blow caught him in the ribs and knocked him sideways off the table. He landed hard on his back and pawed at the air for a few seconds in an effort to get to his feet. Eventually, Moses was able to stand but he immediately hunched over and hissed as the skinny young child ran toward him.

10

Leah was sulking. She didn't want to have a babysitter, she wanted to go to Auntie Linda's and play with Jayne. She was lying on her stomach in the middle of her parents' bed with an open colouring book in front of her; a grinning teddy bear sporting a huge bow tie around its neck stared out from the page. Leah picked up the pink crayon and haphazardly scribbled over the bear and his bow.

"But why can't I go to Jayne's? I'll be good."

"It's not a question of you being good Milady!" Millie was fast losing her patience. "Auntie Linda can't look after you so your Uncle Frank is coming over and that's that!" She tried for the fifth time to get the back on to her earring but it still would not go on. She gave the back a determined shove and finally felt the bar slip into place and hold in the clip.

"Yvonne is coming over too, you like her don't you."

"Yes, she's nice and lets me try her lipstick." Leah had finished ruining the bears smile with a blue crayon and turned the page ready to mutilate a flower and butterfly with more hasty scribbles.

Millie groaned inwardly when she saw the mess Leah was making in her colouring book. ""Does she now? Well don't get any ideas that I will buy you some, you're too young for that."

Millie sprayed her favourite perfume around the base of her neck, the delicate scent of honeysuckle wafted in the air. She patted an errant strand of hair back into place and asked: "How do I look?"

"You look beautiful," a voice replied from the door way. Joe stood and smiled admiringly. His wife was an attractive lady and today she looked extra lovely. She wore her favourite black dress with its matching diamante belt which sparkled as it caught the light. Her hair was held in a clip behind each ear and hung in soft waves down her back. Millie rarely wore make up and when she did it was only to enhance her natural beauty: a little mascara, just a dab of blue eye shadow and the merest hint of dusky pink lipstick.

Millie walked over to him and kissed his cheek, "thank you and you look very handsome."

Joe blushed and shyly ducked his head. He only ever went out to go drinking with his friends from work and he never dressed up for that, but today he wanted to make the extra effort. Fifteen years ago today he had married this beautiful lady beside him and he wanted to celebrate properly and that meant getting dressed up. He'd had his only suit cleaned, been for a haircut at the barbers in town and polished his shoes. Joe didn't feel that his efforts had resulted in anything special, until Millie had called him handsome.

"Ahh," Joe cleared his throat, "when is your Frank supposed to be..." the knock at the door interrupted him "here?"

Millie laughed softly and left to let in Frank and Yvonne, Joe followed behind. Leah stayed on the bed so she could finish butchering the innocent flower with a dark brown crayon.

***

Yvonne was sprawled on the sofa, the TV was on and Green Door by Shakin' Stevens was playing on Top of the Pops, but she couldn't care less. Frank was kissing her like his life depended on it and she could barely breath.

Frank moved his hand down her leg and drew her over to sit astride his lap, all while keeping his mouth firmly planted to hers. She could feel the bulge in his jeans and it spurred her on, but the need for oxygen made her pull away.

Yvonne sat back and stroked his face, his dark hair stuck out at odd angles where she had clung to him. His sky blue eyes stared at her and watched as she pulled her blonde hair away from her neck with one hand and fanned herself with the other. The top three buttons of her blouse were open and Frank could see her full cleavage, flushed and heaving as she breathed deeply. He wanted her.

He grabbed her waist and buried his head in the V her blouse made and kissed her skin. Yvonne squealed in surprise, and then moaned as he began to lick up her neck...

The sudden opening of the living room door behind them startled Frank and he all but threw Yvonne on the seat next to him. He hastily brushed his fingers through his hair and shyly looked over the back of the sofa. Leah stood by the door, her eyes huge and frightened. "Uncle Frank, I heard a noise and I was scared. There's something in my room."

"I'm sure there's nothing to worry about, but let's look and make sure eh?" Frank looked at Yvonne, he wanted to apologise but she was busy re-buttoning her blouse and tucking it back inside her jeans.

"Be back in a couple of minutes love."

"It's alright; she probably just had a bad dream. There won't be anything there." Yvonne looked back at Leah and asked if she was OK. Leah nodded and waited for Frank before going back upstairs. Moses was meowing in the kitchen. "He probably wants feeding." Yvonne said as she got up and went into the kitchen to search for his food.

"Right Mrs!" Frank picked up Leah and swung her round on to his back. He held her ankles and felt her little hands hold on to his shoulders. He stood at the bottom of the stairs, his right foot stroking the ground. "Ready... Three... Two... One... Charge!!!" Leah let out a howl of laughter as Frank bounded up the stairs two at a time.

Yvonne finished emptying the can of food into the bowl and Moses let out a grateful meow and started to eat. Seeing he had hardly any water left, she grabbed his water dish, filled it and set it back down beside him. She stroked him once and stood to wash her hands.

She let the water run over her fingers and smiled as she thought about what had happened in the living room a few moments ago. She was so deep in thought she hadn't heard Frank come into the room and she jumped slightly when she felt his strong fingers on her back. She closed her eyes and leaned forward against the sink as Frank moved his hands down and gave her bottom a squeeze, then trailed his fingers up and around her waist. She could feel his hot breath on her neck so Yvonne let her head roll to the side to give him access. His lips sucked on the exposed skin below her ear and she shivered.

The hands slowly moved up to squeeze her breasts; she moaned and gripped the sink as his fingers kneaded her soft flesh. One hand moved slowly downwards...

"I think you were right, I think it was just a bad dream."

The hands melted away and slowly the realisation dawned that Frank had not been with her this whole time. She started to shake uncontrollably and her knees buckled. Frank ran to her as she collapsed on the floor.

"Baby, what's wrong." Frank reached for her, but before he could touch her, she cried out as though she'd been scalded.

"I have to go!" Yvonne scrambled to her feet and clutched at the sink for support.

"Why? What's happened?" Frank had never seen her behave like this and he was scared.

"Someone molested me!" She wailed.

"When? I don't understand!" He reached for her but she shied away. He held his hands up to show he wasn't going to harm her and listened as she told him what had happened when he had taken Leah back to her room. Her voice was shaky and her eyes looked crazed as she spoke.

"It's not possible."

"I'm not a liar Frank!" She shouted. She looked at him, desperate for some sign that he believed her but there was none. "I'm going, I can't... Wouldn't stay here if you paid me!" Yvonne ran past Frank, he turned and watched her go and couldn't bring himself to reach out and say he believed her when he just didn't know if he did.

11

"Is she still not talking to you?" Millie asked. She leaned back on the sofa and took a long drink from the can of lager.

Frank looked up from behind the TV. "Yeah, we're talking now, but she's still upset with me. She says she can't be with someone who won't believe her. I mean, I know you've had some crazy shit happen in this place, but I can't believe that something groped her." He disappeared from view. "There, that's connected. Now to tune it in."

"She's never lied to you before Frank and I can't see as she would make that up."

Frank grimaced as he stood up and squeezed from behind the TV unit. "No but, it just doesn't seem possible."

Joe's footsteps could be heard coming down the stairs, within moments he walked through the living room door on his way to the kitchen. "Leah's gone to sleep." Joe came back in carrying three unopened cans of lager and put one on the table next to Frank's chair.

"Are you sure Dave doesn't mind us borrowing his VHS?" Joe asked as he plopped down next to Millie on the sofa. He passed a can to her who, having just drained hers, tugged on the ring pull and took a gulp of the cold lager.

"Nah, Dave's fine with it mate." Frank rotated the dial on the front of the TV and after a few moments the screen cleared and the JVC menu appeared. He pressed the eject button and the loading drawer extended from the top of the machine. He took the VHS tape out of its box and slid it into the drawer and pressed it back down. It shut with a soft click and he pressed 'play'. The machine whirred to life and the words 'The Exorcist' flashed on the screen in bright red letters. He rubbed his hands together and went back to his chair. He opened his beer and took a sip.

Millie looked at Frank and laughed. "Mother wouldn't let me see this when it first came out, do you remember? 'You're not watching that in your condition, people have had heart attacks and died ya know!'" There had been reports of people fainting, having seizures and the odd case of someone having a heart attack in the cinemas while watching the film, but that didn't deter Millie, pregnant or not she was going to see it. That was until Ruby convinced Joe to put his foot down and stop her, so to keep the peace she gave up and the film went unwatched.

"Seven years I've waited to see this, it had better be worth it!"

Twenty minutes into the film Millie yawned. "God this is slow!"

"Shh, it'll get better!" Frank grumbled and rolled his eyes.

A short while later, Millie started to really enjoy the film and was deeply engrossed in a scene where Regan was thrashing on her bed as it moved and bucked by an unseen force . The terrified girl on the screen screamed and flopped around like a fish out of water, all the time her distraught mother looked on. The tape suddenly came to a stop. Joe, who was sitting nearest the TV, pressed play on the remote which was connected to the JVC by a meter long cord. The machine whirred again and the petrified Regan resumed her struggle to stay on the bed.

Over the next forty minutes as Regan was drawn deeper into her demonic possession and her interactions with the other characters became more intense, the machine would stop playing at crucial points. With less than twenty minutes to go, the two priests arrived to exorcise the child. Regan sat up in the bed and her head began to rotate and once again the VHS stopped playing, but this time the machine was completely shut off as was the TV set.

"I'm going for more beer." Joe got up and went to the kitchen to grab three more cans.

"Oh for fuck's sake!" Frank jumped out of his chair and pressed the power button on the TV, but it would not come back on. He looked at the VHS player and realised that the timer wasn't illuminated. He leaned over the back of the TV and saw that both the power cords had been removed from the wall socket.

"Err, Millie!" He was shocked by what he saw and didn't know how to rationalise it in his own mind, let alone tell anyone about what he was looking at. "Looks like your ghost doesn't want you to watch this film. The err..." he coughed nervously. "The plugs have been pulled out the wall!"

"You're joking!" Millie joined frank by the TV and looked behind the set to see both black cords lying neatly together on the floor a good six inches from the wall. Frank squeezed back behind the TV and reached for the two plugs. Frank heard the slap before her felt the blow as something knocked his hand away. He recoiled as if he'd been electrocuted and toppled backwards to land awkwardly on his behind.

Millie looked at Frank and raised a single eyebrow. "So when are you going to tell Yvonne you believe her?"

***

It was after 2am and Millie was struggling to sleep. The room was hot and stuffy and they had left their bedroom door wide open to pull the slightest breeze into the room. But even with the landing window and their bedroom windows open, there was still no breeze coming through into the room. Millie had tied her hair back and wore her thinnest night gown, but her neck and chest were drenched in sweat.

She rolled on to her left side and stared through the doorway into the dark landing and mulled over what had happened that evening. There was a rational explanation for the VHS stopping: dust in the motor, the heads needing to be cleaned or even a problem with the cassette. But there was no explaining how the plugs had been removed from the wall.

Frank had pulled the VHS from the TV unit and put it back in its box. He didn't want to risk attempting to plug the thing back in just in case 'Fred', as they had now dubbed the ghost, hit him again. While Frank packed the VHS away Millie plugged the TV back in and it immediately came back on, but no one was in the mood to watch anything so the TV was turned off.

Millie had noticed a bruise forming on Frank's wrist where he'd been hit and offered him some ice for the pain, but he refused saying that it didn't hurt. She and Frank had talked for a while before he left and he'd said: "I just don't know what to make of it. I've always thought this house was strange, but now it's getting violent. Millie love, you seriously need to think about your family's safety!" He'd kissed her and left.

She didn't know what to make of the whole thing. She was shocked by some of the things they'd experienced in the very short time they had lived here, but did they warrant another move in so short a time? Millie didn't think so and she knew Joe would balk at the idea, so she put the thought from her mind and again tried to sleep.

Millie felt her eyelids getting heavy and welcomed it. Her breathing became slow and deep and her eyes closed a once... twice... A light on the stairs instantly made her alert. "Bloody cars! Who in their right mind is out at...." but she couldn't finish the thought as she realised she couldn't hear a car in the street. The light, an ethereal blue glow, slowly moved up the stairs. The hairs on her neck stood up, a shiver ran down her spine and goosebumps formed on her arms. Fright blurred her vision and her breathing became erratic.

Millie's eyes quickly focussed and she watched transfixed as the light took on form. She was able to make out an old man's profile as he softly climbed the stairs and reached the landing at the top. She couldn't see him now, but knew he was still there as the blue glow was still present. The soft footsteps continued along the landing and Millie's heart lurched in her chest. She held her hands to her mouth and said a silent prayer that whoever was there would not see her.

The figure proceeded along the landing with frustrating slowness and eventually appeared and walked in front of her bedroom doorway. He stopped and turned to peer into the room. Millie was desperately trying to keep calm. She wanted to close her eyes, but she felt oddly compelled to look at the old man.

He was nothing but mist below the knees, but the rest of him was crystal clear. He was dressed in dark trousers and a pale shirt with its sleeves rolled up to the elbows to reveal thin arms. He wore a dark waistcoat with a fob chain hanging from a little pocket on his left side, a slight dint in the pocket gave the impression that his watch was still there. He had a grey flat cap perched on the top of his head and round steel rimmed glasses through which Millie could see his eyes with their long white lashes. The old man smiled at Millie and turned to continue his walk along the landing to the small bedroom, the door of which was kept firmly shut.

Millie rushed out of bed and went to the landing. She was aware of two things: the feint smell of black cherry pipe tobacco and the coldness of the air. A shiver ran down her back though and she began to tremble, though whether that was due to the cool air or the shock of seeing the old man she could not say. What she did know with a certainty is that she was now wide awake and likely would not be able to sleep tonight.

12

Saturday August 22nd 1981
10.20am

Millie was sitting in the Dolphin café on Shrewhill High
Street waiting for her mother, a plate covered in toast
crumbs and a half drunk cup of tea sat in front of her on the
table. Unusually the place was empty except for Millie and
the manageress Beverley who was busy wiping tables.

Millie picked up her tea and listened as the transistor
radio behind the counter began to play Ghost Town by The
Specials. She smiled at the irony.

It had happened again. The old man had walked the
landing and had stopped outside the master bedroom and
looked at Millie, but this time she had been asleep. This
time Joe had been the one to see him.

As Millie had predicted she didn't get any sleep
Tuesday night after seeing the Old Man and as soon as Joe
got up she told him exactly what she'd seen. After
everything they had experienced in the few months they had
lived at 33, he didn't believe her. He thought she had had
too much to drink after what had happened with the VHS
player. Millie had been furious, she'd had three cans of lager
and that was piss weak! They had argued and Millie hadn't
spoken to Joe with any civility since then.

This morning as she was getting ready to meet her
mother, Joe had apologised and told her that last night he
had seen the old man standing outside their bedroom. Joe
said that he watched as the old man walked towards the
little bedroom and disappeared through the closed door.
He'd then come to bed and lay awake that night, unable to
sleep. Millie had told him that she had thought about
moving but Joe had flat out refused to consider it. "So the
house had a ghost!" he'd said. "We've been here less than
five months and I'll be damned if I'll move again so soon!"
he'd said.

The door bell jingled announcing that a customer was entering the premises. Millie looked up and spotted her mother just closing the door.

"Hello chick!" Ruby greeted Millie, and then called over: "Bev, can I get two teas please?"

"Of course, sit down, I'll bring them over," Beverley replied.

Ruby brushed the chair with her hand and sat down then finally got a good look at Millie. "Good lord, you look rough! What the hell's the matter?"

"Thanks mother!" Millie rolled her eyes. "I've not been sleeping too well."

Beverley brought over two steaming cups of tea and as they were being drunk Millie told her mother about the recent activity in the house. While Ruby was sceptical by nature she listened intently as Millie told her about the visits from 'Fred'. She also told her mother about the incident with the VHS and how Frank had his hand slapped away when he'd tried to plug it back in.

Ruby had heard about last Tuesday from Frank and she'd seen the bruise on his wrist from the alleged attack, but she found it all incredibly hard to believe. She even thought her brother's letter mysteriously finding its way there had to have a rational explanation. She couldn't think of one off hand, but there had to be one. It was only when she had, by chance, bumped into Yvonne that she finally started to believe that Millie's house really did have a something supernatural inhabiting it.

By the time Millie had finished, the cups were empty and Ruby had smoked several cigarettes.

"What with him next door, it's all been incredibly stressful and I don't know what the hell to do!" Millie frowned and rubbed her forehead.

Ruby had never really been maternal and found it difficult to offer them comfort when her kids were upset, that had always been left to their father but he wasn't here and Millie needed her. She reached over and patted Millie's elbow as it rested on the table. "Millie, I believe you. I didn't want to; it all seemed too far-fetched to be true, but I do believe you. I saw Yvonne a couple of weeks ago and I asked her why she had stopped seeing Frank. She told me what happened at your place. Millie, by the sound of it, none of you are safe there."

"Frank said something to that effect last time I saw him."

"You need to either get help or get out. What if something attacked Leah, you'd never forgive yourself if she got hurt!"

Millie slowly nodded her head in agreement and took her purse from her bag. "You're right, you're both right, but you try telling Joe that! He refuses to move and no matter what I say I just can't convince him that we should leave." She shoved her chair away from the table and went to the counter to settle the bill. She returned shortly after and picked up her handbag and shopping bags and waited while her mother visited the ladies room.

Beverley came over and began to clear their table. She was just about to turn away when she changed her mind and said: "I hope you don't think I was being nosey, but I couldn't help overhearing what you were talking about. My friend Barry is an excellent medium and has helped a few people over the years. I can give you his number if you like."

Millie was about to refuse the offer, but her inner voice told her to get in touch with this guy and see what he had to say. "Thanks Bev, at this point, I'll try anything."

Beverley smiled and trotted back behind the counter. Not long after she returned and pressed a small piece of paper into Millie's hand and wished her luck.

***

2.35pm

"Millie have you seen my wallet? I had it this morning but it's not where I left it." Joe came into the living room and began methodically searching through the

64

drawers in the sideboard, taking all the items out of one drawer and replacing them one by one so he could make sure he didn't miss a thing. "Well?"

"Well what?" Millie was lying curled up on the sofa flicking through the pages of her Kays mail order catalogue and hadn't heard him come in. She spied a pretty two piece blouse and cardigan set and folded the corner over to mark the page.

"Have you seen my wallet?" Joe looked up and saw the catalogue. "Haven't you got enough clothes?"

"No and yes!" Millie threw the catalogue on the sofa and got up to help Joe search.

"Eh?" Joe closed the drawer and moved on to the cupboard below the far right drawer.

"No, I've not seen your wallet and yes, I have enough clothes." She straightened the ornaments that Joe had shoved aside to make room to empty the drawers. She used her sleeve to buff some dust off the large blue ornamental brandy glass and replaced it in the centre of the sideboard.

"Where the hell is it? I'm meeting Tommy at the Tavern later!"

"When did you see it last?" Millie asked. She walked into the kitchen and looked on the mantle above the fireplace, but apart from a few bills that needed paying, the matches to start the fire and her hair brush it was empty. She quickly glanced at the floors in case it had fallen then went back in to the living room and began searching the book cases. Joe finished looking through the cupboards and winced as he stood up.

"I paid the coal man and an hour later the window cleaner came round so I had it then to pay him and I left it on the fireplace in the kitchen but it's not there!"

"Leah wouldn't have moved it would she?"

"No she's been round the Pember's since you left to go shopping." Joe walked round to the sofa and dropped down heavily. He rubbed his face and looked at Millie who had come to sit with him on the sofa. "Where the hell is it?" He sighed and looked up at the ceiling. In a loud voice he yelled: "FRED! BRING MY WALLET BACK RIGHT NOW, I NEED IT!"

Joe glanced over at Millie and they both started to laugh. He shrugged, "it was worth a try!"

Their laughter was cut short by a sudden swishing noise which emanated from the sideboard. They both looked over the back of the sofa and stared in disbelief as Joe's wallet was swirling around inside the large blue brandy glass as though it was being pushed by someone or something they could not see. They continued to watch as the wallet lost its momentum and slid to a halt in the bottom of the glass.

Joe rushed to the sideboard and fished his wallet out from the glass and was surprised to discover that it was ice cold. He swallowed nervously and croaked out a very quiet "thank you".

"Joe I think we should get help with this place. Bev at the café gave me the number of someone she thinks might be able to explain what's going on or even help us to get rid of it."

Millie went to her bag the hall and grabbed the piece of paper Beverley had shoved in her hand that morning. She read the paper and said: "his name's Barry and apparently he's a very good psychic."

"I don't know Mill. I don't really believe in all that stuff."

"Are you kidding me? The things you've seen, all the times you've lost stuff just to find them again somewhere else. Your bloody wallet just appeared out of thin air for god's sake!" She waved the piece of paper at his wallet to highlight her point. "After all that, you're questioning whether someone can talk to the thing that's doing all this!"

Suddenly a loud thumping began on the walls making the pictures shake and the ornaments rattle. Then from the hall they heard a child laugh and footsteps quickly climbing the stairs. Millie turned and ran after the noise, taking the steps two at a time. She reached the landing and saw the attic hatch above her head flip up into the air as though it had been punched out of the way.

66

She was scared and angry. Her heart raced and it wasn't just from running full pelt up the stairs. Mustering her courage she yelled: "STOP!" Instantly the thumping ceased.

Joe appeared behind her and pulled her into his arms. He kissed the top of her head and whispered: "call them."

13

Wednesday September 2nd 1981
2.15pm

"Leah please, keep the noise down!" Millie sighed. "I'm sorry about that, please go on."

"I'd like to pay a visit to your home if that would be OK? I'm not available until next Monday, will that suit you?" The man's voice crackled down the line.

"Yes, that's perfect. What time would you be able to come over, I'm at work until 4pm."

"I can be there at 6."

"That would be fine. I can't thank you enough."

"Let's see if we can help you. If we can, then you can thank us." The voice laughed. *"Mrs Holden, I want to be clear that while I can communicate with spirit and I try to help them move on, such things can often be unsuccessful."*

"I understand. I look forward to seeing you on Monday. Goodbye Mr Haynes."

"Goodbye Miriam." The line clicked as the voice hung up.

Millie sat there holding the receiver in stunned silence. She hadn't told him her full name, just started the conversation with: "Hello, my name is Millie Holden..."

"Sorry for being noisy mummy." Leah was standing in front of her mother and looked concerned. "Mummy are you OK?"

"What? Oh yes, I'm fine." She dropped the receiver back on the cradle and looked at her daughter. "As for the noise, you know I always ask you to be quiet when I'm on the phone. What was all the fuss about?"

"I was singing along to the radio and dancing."

"Oh right, going to be a pop star are we?" Millie smiled. Times never changed, she did exactly the same thing when she was Leah's age.

Leah laughed and ran back into the kitchen, her hair swung from side to side in the ponytail on the top of her head.

Millie sat back and listened as the knocking started on the ceiling. Since Joe's wallet had disappeared they had experienced banging noises of various degrees. Sometimes the pipes would rattle, other times what sounded like feet would walk across the bedroom floors and on occasion there would be three loud raps on the windows. The lights had also started to flicker on and off for no apparent reason and still the airing cupboard door and attic hatch could be found open after they had been shut. There had been no more sightings of Fred or the red eyes in the bathroom, which Millie was thankful for.

She had hoped to speak to Barry Haynes, Beverley's psychic friend, almost two weeks ago, but today was the first day he had actually answered the phone. When he picked up the phone and Millie told him she had been trying to contact him, he was extremely contrite and explained that he and his wife had been away at a seminar in Devon and only recently returned. Millie didn't mind, she was just happy that he understood her concerns about the house and seemed genuinely willing to help.

What she was less than happy about was Jellyman next door. Over the past few weeks he had been flying his pigeons more frequently and the blasted things kept crapping on her laundry. It was almost like he waited for her to peg out her washing so he could then let out his birds. Last Sunday she had a line full of sheets and Leah's new school clothes, she had watched in horror as the birds were promptly released and had wasted no time in using her clean laundry for target practice. She had called to him over the hedge and asked him, as polite as she possibly could given her mood, not to let his birds out when he could see she had washing to dry. He had yelled back: "Mind your own fuckin' business!" and disappeared into the house.

There were also times when he opened the bin by the hedge and the smell from the rotting corpses inside would infiltrate their house. Some of the neighbours in the street had cats go missing and Millie was convinced that if someone had the stomach to check the bin in Jellyman's garden, their beloved pets would be found in there.

The banging upstairs finally stopped and Millie sighed in relief. She looked at the clock and realised Joe would be home from work soon and dinner was still in the fridge. Millie was off this week having taken some of her holiday time so she could finish getting Leah ready for school. The new school year was due to start next Monday and she still needed a new bag and some stationary. They had planned a shopping trip to Birmingham on Friday so they could buy the rest of her essentials.

Millie walked into the kitchen and headed straight for the fridge to grab the sausages she'd bought this morning. She quickly threw the sausages on the oven pan and turned on the oven.

"Leah can you get me the potatoes out the pantry please?" Millie got the huge stainless steel pot and filled it with water. A few minutes later she was sitting at the kitchen table, peeling potatoes and singing along to the 60's music playing on the radio. Leah was sitting opposite her in another desperate struggle to un-knot her dolls long black hair.

***

She was doing it again. It had been happening for weeks now and he was sick of it. Every time he was out flying his birds, the brat from next door was watching him. Didn't those stupid people next door teach their kid it was rude to stare? He'd bloody show her.

He thought he'd taught her a lesson a couple of months ago when she and that loud mouth friend of hers were playing in the back yard and screaming like they were being slaughtered. He'd yelled and they'd gone back in, but of course the mouthy cow from next door had the cheek to moan at him for making them stop. He'd bloody show her an' all one day!

The night after the little shits had been screaming he'd collected all the glass bottles he had stored in the cubby hole under the stairs and broke it into decent sized pieces. Then he'd sneaked to the bottom of his garden and managed to pull the hedge away from the back fence just enough to allow him to squeeze through. He'd cut himself laying the glass down on that stupid hill they had in the back yard, but it was worth it to stop the dark haired brat from playing there. He'd heard the commotion from their back garden and knew one of the little shits had hurt themselves; he didn't care which one as long as they stopped their racket and his birds were content.

***

Joe was standing in Millie's veggie garden watering the plants. He had finished his dinner and was full to bursting. Millie was a great cook and made sure that whoever she cooked for was sated. This afternoon there had been sausages, mashed potatoes, cauliflower and gravy and Millie had even made Yorkshire puddings. Joe was not a domineering husband who demanded his dinner be ready for him when he got home, but he was always grateful when it was. Unlike his sister Doris' husband who demanded to be waited on hand a foot. How she put up with that tyrant he never knew. They'd argued many times over George's treatment of her, but Doris didn't listen and had cut Joe off without so much as a 'goodbye'. He loved his sister and didn't want to see her come to any harm, but what could he do if she didn't want to speak to him.

Joe shrugged off the thought and turned back to fill his watering can from the rainwater barren by the kitchen window. He had barely stepped two paces when he noticed the net curtain in Leah's bedroom twitch. He watched as the face he had seen so many times peered out of the window and studied Jellyman's pigeons as they circled the houses beyond their respective gardens. The child in the window looked sad and lonely and terribly in need of food. The eyes

71

were small dots surrounded by dark circles, the cheeks were sunken in and the skin was the colour of tallow.

The child leaned forward and pressed against the window as though to get a better view of Jellyman's garden next door and Joe could see the child was naked. Her ribs were clearly visible and her stomach was concave. The child was little more than a skeleton.

Joe was startled by a loud screech from next door. "FUCKIN' SCUMBAG! STOP STARING AT ME!" Jellyman shouted. A clump of dirt sailed over the hedge and hit their kitchen window with a solid thud. The emaciated child in the upstairs window began to laugh.

Joe shouted: "Hey! What do you think you're doing?" He dropped the watering can and ran towards the house just as Millie came around the corner with Leah trailing in her wake. Joe picked her up and walked back indoors. Jellyman shouted another curse and lump of soil flew across the hedge, this time it hit its mark. Dirt and grass exploded on Leah's bedroom window to rain down on Millie who was fast approaching the hedge.

"What in the name of God is wrong with you?" Millie climbed on the pile of wood that was still sitting in the corner of the yard and opened a gap in the hedge to peer through.

Jellyman spotted her and waved a dirty finger in the direction of the upstairs window. "That bastard brat of yours is in that window upstairs staring at me again and I've had enough!" His face was almost purple he was so angry, which did nothing to improve his looks.

"You're deranged. My child was helping me wash up; we've been there at least twenty minutes. Not that I need explain anything to the likes of you!"

"Lie all you want to wench, but I know what I saw. That nosey bastard is always watching me and laughing. That's harassment and if you allow her to keep doing it, I'll call the police." He coughed and spit on the floor.

Millie shook her head. "You're mistaken, I don't know what you think you're seeing but it definitely isn't my child."

72

Jellyman puffed out his chest and was about to say something but Millie cut him off before he could start on her again.

"You're old and possibly a bit senile so I'm going to make allowances for that, but I will tell you once more... we have one child and she has been with me this whole time." Millie started to close the gap in the hedge, but opened them so swiftly Jellyman was caught by surprise, the look on his face was comical and Millie almost burst out laughing. "Don't ever throw anything at my house again do you hear old man? Any more nonsense from you and I'll let the neighbours know where they can find their poor cats!" She nodded towards the bin by the side of the hedge and for once Jellyman looked uncomfortable.

14

Thursday September 3rd 1981
12.25pm

The house stank of something unmentionable; almost a cross between food that had been digested and regurgitated and a rotting carcass, but the occupant was oblivious to it. The once brightly decorated walls were now a stained with mildew and nicotine from years of chain smoking and a brown film clung to everything throughout the property.

The bedrooms fared no better and were filled from floor to ceiling with old newspapers and boxes of mouldy clothes and shoes. The stairs were also stacked with newspapers leaving barely enough room for anyone to navigate them safely. The living room was somewhat cleaner, but that was mainly due to the occupant spending most of their time either in their bedroom or in the kitchen.

The kitchen was also filthy. A stack of plates rested precariously on the draining board after they had been half heartedly washed and rinsed under the cold tap. The floor was piled with dirty laundry and something furry was rummaging through the open bags of refuse stacked in the corner by the pantry. A brown leather chair, stained and ripped from years of use, sat by the fire place, it creaked as Victor Jellyman stood up.

The front door had just been knocked and he knew by the three sharp raps that his sister Doreen had left his shopping by the back gate. He had little time for his sister and she made it abundantly clear that she detested him, but out of family loyalty she still cared for him by collecting his pension, paying his bills and buying his shopping. Doreen flat out refused to enter the house and left all of his supplies by the back gate for him to collect after she had gone.

His sister was younger than him by fourteen years; having been born four months after their father had joined up in 1915. He had been born in 1901 the day after Queen Victoria died and had been christened Victor in her

74

memory. Their father had been killed during the Battle of Passchendaele and Victor became the breadwinner of the family. He couldn't remember much about his dad, apart from loud voice and feel of his belt when he'd had too much to drink. Victor didn't shed a single tear when his mother read the telegram. Good riddance to bad rubbish, he wouldn't miss the violent drunken bastard.

By 1935 Doreen was married and living in her own home. Victor continued to live with his mother and in 1939, on the cusp of World War II, they moved from their old dilapidated miner's house to this newly built property. Victor's mother died in 1942 and he was devastated. He became increasingly reclusive and as time went on he stopped caring about himself or the property. Slowly over the years they became the stinking wrecks they were today.

Victor came back from outside with the haul that Doreen had left by the gate, bread, milk, sugar, tea, cheese and ham for sandwiches and several slabs of cake from the bakery where Doreen still worked on the High Street. He grabbed a dirty knife from the counter and opened the plastic wrapper on a moist cherry cake. He cut a chunk and wandered back outside to visit his birds.

The shed where the pigeons were housed was immaculate when compared to his house. Victor spent most of his daylight hours cleaning the floor of guano, feeding and exercising his birds. He had learned how to care for pigeons from his father, about the only decent thing that old fool had done, and the skill had never left him. He had even raced pigeons in his younger years but as he got older he stopped going out and just contented himself with breeding them and letting them fly around the neighbourhood.

He opened the shed door and a mass of feathers and cooing noises erupted from the doorway and took to the skies. Victor looked inside the shed and saw one bird sitting on the floor, one of its wings hung loosely at its side and it struggled to walk. It lurched forward as Victor reached down and picked it up, the creature bobbed its head and cooed as he petted it. Victor shuffled back outside and grasped the bird by the feet and swung it at the corner of the shed. The bird flapped its good wing in a feeble effort to escape and shrieked as its neck connected solidly to the wood. He swung it twice more for good measure then took its carcass to the bin he kept by the hedge and threw it in with the rest of the animals he'd dispatched over the last few months.

Victor looked up at the hedge and grumbled to himself. "Bastard had no right to cut that hedge." The skinny bloke from next door had cut it once and had trimmed another six inches off it recently. He could almost see the top of their kitchen window. He didn't want them nosing into his garden, it was bad enough hearing the kids playing outside without seeing them an' all.

He looked up at their house and a movement in the upstairs window caught his attention. The net curtain moved and the face of a child looked out. He watched the face follow his birds as they flew over the garden and circled the houses in Mill Place. Slowly the child looked down and stared intently at him making him feel uncomfortable. Victor coughed and spat on the ground all the while he kept his focus on the window. The face broke into what he supposed was a smile but then it began to contort and he knew the child was laughing at him. He growled in anger. "Nosey bastard, fuck off!" But his outburst made the child laugh all the harder.

Victor growled in anger and stalked towards the house, then stopped suddenly. He slowly smiled as he remembered that he'd seen the couple from next door leave the house when he collected his shopping from the back gate. They had left their kid alone in the house, it didn't seem possible, but he had definitely seen their brat in the upstairs window. He chuckled to himself and carried on walking to the house, he saw an opportunity that he just couldn't pass up.

***

5pm

"Leah, don't run too far in front!" Joe called out. Leah immediately stopped and waited for her parents. She was happy and excited to get home so she could show Jayne the new doll her nanny had bought for her. Leah had spent last night at her nanny's house and her parents had come to collect her that afternoon. They'd had lunch and played in the back garden while the sun shone brilliantly overhead.

Millie and Joe quickly caught up to her. They each took one of her hands and waited for the traffic to ease so they could cross the Burntwood Road. The last car had passed them and the three quickly crossed the road and turned into New Street which led down to Baggott's Circle. Leah raced on ahead leaving her parents to follow on at their own pace. Millie and Joe usually let her run by herself as they were so near to home and more than once they found her waiting by the back gate of the house.

"What's she doing?" Millie said. Joe looked at her then looked ahead to look for Leah. She was standing at the corner of Baggott's Circle, staring into the street. She turned and pointed down the street, she looked back to her parents who were less than ten feet away.

"There's a police car mummy! Outside our house!"

"What they hell do they want?" Joe picked up Leah and started to jog towards home with Millie following quickly behind.

They made short work in reaching their home and arrived to find a police car and a strange black Ford Escort parked in front of their house. There were also several neighbours in the street watching as Joe, Millie and Leah were about to walk down their garden path but were stopped by a tall police officer.

"Excuse me Sir, Madam. But could you wait here please?" The officer said, holding his hand out to keep them from going down the path.

"Why, what's the matter officer?" Joe put Leah on the ground. She immediately stepped behind her mother and looked up with huge eyes.

A lady came to stand in front of Joe. "Mr Holden, my name is June Myatt, I'm from social services. We have received a complaint that you have left a child alone in the house. The complainant said the child looked malnourished. We will need your keys so we can check the validity of the claim."

"What utter rubbish!" Millie called out. "She has been with us all day." She dragged Leah to stand in front of her. "Does she look malnourished to you?" Millie was angry and her voice rose in volume as she spoke.

The lady looked taken aback by Millie's attitude and the new information she had received, but undeterred she continued: "Your keys Mr Holden." She held out her hand and waited while Joe dug his set of keys out of his pocket.

"This is bloody ridiculous. Ask any of our neighbours and they will all tell you we have one child and we would never harm a hair on her head." Millie had been angry before but now she was irate.

"Madam, I will have to ask you to keep calm while this is sorted out." The police officer spoke softly which did nothing to calm Millie. She watched impotently as the lady and a second policeman, who had been standing by the front door all this time, entered the property and disappeared from view.

June and the officer walked in and made a quick scan of the kitchen and living room before heading upstairs to check the rooms up there. All the doors were closed tight apart from the attic hatch which was out of alignment, but they discounted looking there as it was too high for child to reach. They looked in the bathroom and the small front bedroom which was so full of boxes no one would get in there, not even a skinny kid. Next they looked in the master bedroom leaving the back bedroom, where the caller had said he'd seen the child, till last.

June turned the door knob and pushed but the door was stuck fast. She pushed again and still it would not budge. She looked to the officer and motioned for him to help her get the door open. Her heart was pounding and all manner of horrors raced through her mind. She'd seen some terrible things in her years of child protection and she dared not think what state the poor child was in on the other side of the door.

Finally the door opened and they burst into the room. June and the policeman stared at each other in bemusement. The room, like all the others in the house, was empty.

Millie was sitting on the curb in front of the Pember's house talking with Joe and Linda. Leah was sitting a few feet away brushing the hair of her new doll, completely oblivious to the drama unfolding around her.

"Mrs Holden?" Millie stood up and faced the owner of the voice. The lady, Myatt or what ever her name was, could barely look at Millie as she continued: "we've finished our walk through the house; we won't be taking any further action."

"Did you find anything?" Millie smirked as June shook her head.

"No and I'm very sorry for any distress this may have caused. Someone was either mistaken or was making a joke at your expense." June held out the set of keys and winced slightly as Millie snatched them out of her fingers.

Out the corner of her eye Millie saw the upstairs curtains move in Jellyman's house and she instantly knew the culprit. "Yes it would appear so!"

15

Monday September 7th 1981
5.50pm

A bright blue Austin Allegro sat outside 33; the occupants were an older couple, a petite lady with curly silver hair and a gentleman of a stocky build with short dark blonde hair. They sat together in the front seats holding hands and saying the same protection prayer they used when entering a haunted property.

Joe came to stand beside Millie and watched the old couple climb out of the car and push the doors shut. "Leah's round Linda's place. I said I'd collect her when they've gone. Will you be OK?" Millie turned towards him and nodded. He kissed her cheek and left her to wait for the couple. "I'll be in the garden if you need me."

Millie watched from the window as the pair began to walk down the path. The lady stopped suddenly and opened the notepad she carried and for almost a minute she scribbled frantically, she turned the page and continued to scribble.

A sharp rap on the door startled Millie and she quickly ran to answer it. "Hello, Mrs Holden, I'm Barry we spoke on the phone last week. This is the wife," he turned to introduce the lady, "Ellen. I hope you don't mind her coming along, she's a brilliant psychic artist and I'm sure her talents will prove useful." Ellen blushed at her husband's praise and greeted Millie.

"Lovely to meet you, please come in. Can I get you both a cup of tea? Or coffee?" Millie walked to the living room and Ellen followed, Barry was still inside the hallway looking intently up the stairs.

"Could we have water please, if it's not too much trouble?" Ellen asked as she sat on the sofa.

"There's a strange feeling emanating from the stairs." Barry came into the living room and sat on the chair by the window which gave him a perfect view of the bottom of the stairs through the open door way.

"Here you go; I put ice in it for you." Millie handed a glass to Ellen who gratefully took a glass and sipped the contents. Millie crossed the short distance to Barry and handed him a glass, which he took and held in his hands.

"Thank you Millie." He smiled and waited for her to sit on the sofa. "I should explain how we are going to approach this. I would like to have a solo walk around the property, with your permission of course, so I can get a feel for the place and attempt to make contact with whomever might be residing here." Barry took a sip of the cool water, small droplets of condensation ran down the glass and across his fingers, but he paid them no attention.

"I will try to ascertain if they are malevolent and should that be the case, I will advise that we perform a smudging to try and cleanse the atmosphere. If Ellen is able to connect with the energy here, she may be able to draw them so we can get a better understanding of who is here or if you have any family that may be around you."

"I have picked up on someone, but I would like to wait to show you the sketch until Barry has finished his walk around so I don't influence him unduly." Ellen took another gulp of the water and set the glass on the floor beside the sofa.

"That all seems perfectly fine."

"If you don't mind, I would like to get started." Barry stood up and took out the angel talisman he kept for protection and left the ladies together. He closed the living room door behind him and began to climb the stairs.

The air was cooler on the stairs and felt increasingly colder with each step he climbed. He had reached the mid-point of the staircase when a noise above and to the left of him caught his attention. He looked up and saw the attic hatch was ajar. He closed his eyes and quietly asked for the entity to show itself. He had been a psychic medium for the better part of thirty years, but there was still something creepy about being alone in a haunted place that unnerved him.

Barry opened his eyes and looked again at the attic hatch, it hadn't moved and neither had the entity appeared. He held the angel talisman tighter and climbed to the top of the stairs and asked in a louder voice. "I ask you, in the name of our Father God, show yourselves. Let me see you and help you to move on from this place."

The bedroom door directly in front of him moved slightly and he heard a child giggle from inside the room. Something banged in the room to his right taking him by surprise. He gingerly pushed the door open and discovered that this was the bathroom. The airing cupboard was wide open; the door was swinging slightly indicating that it had been opened recently and with some considerable force.

Barry entered the bathroom and looked inside the dark recesses of the airing cupboard. There was nothing but a stack of towels at the front, but he wanted to get a closer look at the back. He grabbed his lighter out of his pocket and flicked the flint wheel a few times to get it to light. After the third flick the flint sparked and a tiny flame appeared. He pushed his hand inside the cupboard to see if anything was lurking in the dark, when a sharp pain on the back of his hand made him gasp and drop the lighter. He yanked his hand back and saw three long red welts along all four of his knuckles, with one being so deep it was beginning to bleed. "You are a nasty little blighter aren't you?" A hiss came from the depths of the airing cupboard making Barry step back and bump into the toilet behind him. He lost his balance and fell back onto the toilet seat, at the same time his lighter flew from the cupboard, hitting the wall opposite before falling into the bath with a resounding clang.

Barry stood up and reached for his talisman and silently prayed to his guides for protection and healing. He picked up his lighter, which he discovered was freezing cold, and left the room. Back out in the hall he was shocked to see two spirits standing on the landing. The first was an older gentleman, dressed in '30's clothing, with white hair and a genuinely welcoming smile on his face.

Standing beside older man was a painfully thin young boy, naked as the day he was born, with shoulder length hair and deeply recessed eyes. The boy unnerved Barry and the energy he projected was identical to the 'thing' in the bathroom.

Barry looked at the young boy and quietly recited his prayer of protection then added: "Divine and Heavenly Father, help this child find peace. Send him love and surround him with your healing light. I ask all this in your name, which is Eternal Love. Amen!" The boy's eyes became brilliant spots of red in the darkened sockets and his face contorted in a bizarre parody of a smile. Barry watched in fascination as the boy dashed straight up into the attic space above him, the hatch rattled then slowly slid back across the hole until it was firmly in place.

The older gentleman was still in his place smiling kindly at Barry and seemed not at all phased by the malevolent force that was a moment ago standing beside him.

16

Monday September 7th 1981
7.20pm

"How did you meet your husband?" Millie sipped her fresh cup of tea.

"We attended the same spiritualist church over in Birmingham, must have been..." Ellen's brow wrinkled in concentration, "thirty years ago. I joined an open circle that Barry was chairing..."

"What's an open circle?" Millie interrupted, then quickly apologised for cutting Ellen off.

"It's a meeting where you try to develop your intuition. Those who are able to develop can go on to train as mediums and then demonstrate at Sunday Service." Ellen looked at Millie intently. "You have a strong energy about you, have you ever considered developing your gift?"

Millie laughed. "No, I've had a couple of weird experiences, some people might call it intuition, but I don't think I would call it a 'gift'."

Ellen was about to protest when the living room door opened and Barry walked into the room. He absent-mindedly rubbed his injured hand as he came round the sofa to sit in the chair by the window.

Ellen noticed the dark red welts and spots of blood on his knuckles. "What happened to your hand?" She started to get up but he waved her back into her seat. "It's nothing. Something disapproved of me intruding on their space." He reached for his glass of water and took a long drink then sat his glass back on the windowsill.

"Ohh that's better!" He sighed in appreciation then turned his gaze on Millie who was patiently waiting to hear what had happened. "Millie, I'm sure you're aware that you have two spirits in your home. There is an older gentleman who tells me that he farmed a piece of land here back at the turn of the century. He had been here for a good number of years and was very upset to have to give up the land for these houses."

Barry closed his eyes and tilted his head as though listening to someone. "He also tells me you remind him of his daughter and he has often watched you sleep." Millie balked at that idea. While she didn't mind the old man being around, she wasn't keen on the idea of him watching her; that was unnerving to say the least. Did he watch her in the bath too?

"He also said that he is keeping your daughter safe from the other one who resides here."

"Is Leah in danger?"

Barry leaned forward in his seat and looked at Millie intently. "I don't want to frighten you, but I have to tell you that there is a dark presence in this house. It is angry and vengeful and thrives on causing mischief. It likes to appear as a young boy and I get the impression that many people over the years have seen this boy. He is a nasty character that likes to hide in dark corners, especially the cupboard in your bathroom. I tried looking in there earlier and got this for my trouble." Barry raised his right hand to illustrate his point.

"The back bedroom is where the 'boy' spends a lot of his time. When I entered the room I sensed a great deal of negative energy and I get the impression that some genius used a Ouija board in there at some point. It is not a pleasant room and I wouldn't be at all surprised if satanic worship took place in there."

Millie put a hand to her mouth in surprise. "Oh my god. When we first moved in we discovered pentagrams carved on the wall in that room. Leah said at the time that she saw the room breathing. We found that the markings on the wall had been filled with white plaster to make them stand out, but they weren't flat and the paper wasn't sticking properly. We managed to get the paper to stick back down and Leah doesn't know what we found."

"Is that the wall that joins to the bathroom?" Barry asked. He reached for his glass and drained the contents.

"Yes!" Millie nodded her head vigorously.

"It's my belief that someone opened a portal and invited the entity in. I don't believe that the entity is a child, but something using that guise to trick people into thinking it's benign. Do I think it's a demon? No. Do I think it's malicious? That would be a definitive yes. It's probable that the person using the Ouija board dearly regretted their actions but didn't know how get rid of the entity, let alone how to close the portal."

Barry looked directly at Ellen and said: "How many times have we had to deal with this?"

"Too many to count." She shook her head and patted Millie's arm. "People play with those things like they're playing Monopoly, but there far more at stake than a couple of fake bank notes!"

"It's my belief," Barry continued, "that the portal is somewhere behind the airing cupboard in your bathroom and the entity uses that as a means to enter and exit the portal. That would explain why the door is constantly opened after you shut it and why it defends the space so vigorously. I saw it enter the attic so it probably lurks there as well, do you hear things up there?"

"The attic hatch is always out of place. We put it back but it's moved again sometime after. We don't go up there though so he can have that space all to himself. I have to ask, can you get rid of it?" Millie asked, her tone hopeful.

"I will give it my best shot, but I can't give you a cast iron guarantee that the thing will be dealt with. It's possible the activity could end completely, or even increase in severity. He's a strong force and it's having too much fun teasing your neighbour." Barry set his glass back on the windowsill and sat back in his chair.

"How do you mean?"

"When I was in the back bedroom, I sensed the 'boy' standing by the window laughing at someone next door. Has your neighbour said anything to you about it?"

"Several times, but he swore black was blue that the child he saw was my daughter. There was once he got quite angry when I told him Leah was with me. Someone called social services and told them we'd left our daughter at home and that she looked starving, I believe it was him next door. I had started to think he was losing his marbles." Millie chuckled to herself, but then a thought occurred to her. "I still don't understand why would he say he saw Leah if you say it's a boy upstairs?"

"The entity has shoulder length hair but it is unmistakably male. He also looks as though he is starving."

Ellen leaned forward in her seat and passed her notepad to Barry. "Is this the boy? I sensed a child in one of the upstairs windows watching us as we walked down the path, so I sketched him."

Barry took the pad and nodded as he recognised the face he'd seen upstairs. "Yes that's the child. Excellent work as always my dear." Barry smiled to his wife and passed the pad to Millie.

Millie looked at the drawing with a strange mixture of disbelief, horror and empathy. The gaunt face of a young boy with shoulder length hair stared out from the page. His eyes were nothing but dark empty sockets in a sunken face. Ellen had skilfully depicted the look of a child on the brink of starvation and Millie was appalled. If she had seen this child in the window, she would have called social services too.

"If you turn the page, you will see another spirit I sensed before we entered the property." Millie turned the page and looked at another well drawn sketch, this time of an older gentleman whose face was as recognisable as her own. The image blurred as her eyes filled with tears. Millie hastily wiped her eyes and looked again at the smiling face on the page. Beside the face were two words: Medicine and Letter. "I take it you know who the gentleman is?" Ellen asked.

Millie wiped her eyes again and nodded. "It's my father. He's been gone a little over three years."

"I'm sorry my dear, I didn't mean to upset you. His presence is very strong around you and I feel he often visits. You'll notice the two words, I heard them very plain, but couldn't discern any meaning to them. Have you any idea what they refer to?"

Millie laughed, her eyes sparkling with tears. "I know exactly what they mean. The day we moved in here I lost my pills and searched all night for them. I got up the next morning and they were all laid out for me on the shelf." She pointed to the mantel shelf above the gas fire in front of her. "I think the 'letter' refers to a letter that my mother received from her brother that found its way here before she had chance to bring it. Dad knew mother had a bad memory, maybe he wanted to make sure I got to read it." Millie smiled and handed the book back to Ellen. "Thank you so much."

Ellen tore out the two drawings and gave them back to Millie. "Keep these, especially the one of your father, with my love and his."

"Well Millie, I think we have taken up too much of your time. I would like to go round the property and offer a blessing if I may and see if we can't get the entity to move on. I will try to get the older gentleman to move on too, but my prime concern is the 'boy'."

Barry stood up and was about to walk to the stairs but he stopped and listened. "The gentleman says you call him 'Fred'?"

Millie burst out laughing. "Yes. It was my husband's idea."

Barry smiled and said: "He likes it!" He continued towards the stairs when Millie's voice called to him. "I'm sorry but I have to ask, how could our neighbour have seen a young girl if you claim it's a boy we have upstairs?"

"Well as I said, he has shoulder length hair so it would be easy for anyone seeing the entity from a distance to assume they were seeing a girl."

"But... How can 'you' be sure that you saw a boy and not a girl?"

"Because my dear, the child is naked."

17

Monday September 7th 1981
7.50pm

Joe was still staring at the piece of paper Millie had passed to him. He had no idea how long he'd been looking at it... Was it ten seconds or ten minutes? He didn't really care; he was too transfixed by the hastily sketched, but skilful, image of a young child. He dropped the paper on to the kitchen table and pushed it away, but he could not stop looking at it.

"Barry said someone used a Ouija board upstairs and it came through and it won't leave."

"Really?" Joe mumbled, not quite paying attention.

"He reckons that it's tormenting that old swine next door. Apparently, it likes to look through Leah's bedroom window and watch him. And, he also said it appeared to be naked, that's how he realised it's a boy. That's horrid isn't it?"

Joe sat up in his chair when Millie mentioned the child being in the window. "I've seen it Millie... a few times and that psychic fella is right, it did look naked. The last time I saw it was when him next door said Leah was staring at him. I'll be honest, the first time I saw it I thought it was Leah too."

"Why have you never told me? You heard what I said to that old fool!" Millie shoved her chair away from the table and stood up in agitation.

Joe's chair scraped along the floor as he got up and rounded the table. He reached out and rested his hands on Millie's shoulders. "I didn't want to worry you. It was bad enough thinking we just had Fred 'round here, but the ghost of a child too, a naked one at that, who likes to hang out in Leah's room. I thought it best not to say anything unless you had seen it too. I'm sorry."

Joe pulled Millie close for a hug. He smiled when her arms wrapped tightly round him.

Millie sighed. "Barry seems to think it's not really a child, but is pretending to be one so it can fool people into thinking it's harmless."

"Oh good lord, how are we supposed to deal with that?"

"He blessed the house and said a few prayers for protection. He didn't know if that would be enough though, but we can but hope eh?" Millie shivered slightly and feeling the involuntary movement, Joe slowly rubbed his hands up and down her back.

"You OK love?" Joe asked. Millie nodded and looked up at him. Joe bent his head down to kiss her upturned lips but after a few seconds he pulled away. "I love you Mrs. But unfortunately there's another little lady I need to see right now."

"Who?" Millie pulled away and cocked an eyebrow at him.

"Wench, have you forgotten about your daughter?" Joe laughed and danced away from her as she playfully swatted his arm.

"Oh get away with you!" She joined in his laughter. Joe blew her a kiss and ran out the door as a tea towel sailed at his head.

Millie was still smiling as she busied herself with collecting the glasses Barry and Ellen had used from the living room. She dropped them in the kitchen sink and ran the hot water so she could wash them. Millie started humming to herself as she walked to the table and pushed the chairs back under it. She grabbed their mugs and immediately stopped humming. It was gone. The picture of the boy should have been sitting in the middle of the table where Joe had left it, but it wasn't there.

Millie dropped the mugs back down with a clatter and bent down to look under the table but it was not there. She checked the chairs and still couldn't see the piece of paper. Joe didn't have it, she'd seen him put it down and shove it away from himself. Millie was on her hands and knees still frantically looking for the piece of paper when Joe and Leah came back in through the back door.

"Hello mummy! Have you lost something?" Leah was standing holding her doll.

"Nothing that can't wait." Millie smiled and stood up. She rubbed the sore spots on her knees and straightened. "Did you have a nice time at Auntie Lin's?"

Leah's face broke out in a huge smile, but it was hard to miss the gap in the top set of teeth. "Yes. I was playing in Jayne's room and look mummy!" Leah held out her hand, a small white tooth lay in the centre of her palm.

Millie groaned inwardly, but used her most cheerful tone: "You know what that means?"

"TOOTH FAIRY!" Leah called out.

"Hooray!" Joe rolled his eyes and walked into the front room.

Millie looked at the clock, it was almost 8:15pm and it was a school night. "Right Milady, it's bed time for you."

Leah pouted and was about to ask to stay up a little longer, but then she remembered her tooth. "If I put my tooth under my pillow will the tooth fairy come? How much do you think I'll get?"

"You'll get nothing if you don't get to bed and put it under your pillow!" Joe shouted from the living room.

***

"Shh, you'll wake her!" Millie stood in their bedroom door way and watched as Joe slowly crept into Leah's room. It was after midnight so she should be fast asleep and Leah was a deep sleeper just like her dad, but Millie was paranoid the slightest movement might wake her and ruin the illusion of a visit from Ye Olde Tooth Faerie.

Joe tiptoed towards Leah's bed; the light from their room illuminated the bed with a soft yellow glow giving him plenty of light to make his way there quietly. Leah was lying on her back with one arm covering her eyes, her soft breaths sounded slow and deep.

Joe took one step forward and the floorboard creaked. He instantly looked at the bed to see if he had woken Leah, but she gave no sign of hearing him or the ghastly noise the floor made. She startled him by coughing. He instantly crouched down and waited to see if she would waken, but she rolled to her left side and curled up in a foetal position. He looked back at the door and saw Millie waving her hand at him, urging him on.

Joe was right by the bed and could easily reach the pillow. He lifted it slowly with his left hand and slid his right hand underneath ready to leave the shiny fifty pence coin and take the tooth. He dropped the coin and felt around for a second until he felt not only the tiny baby tooth, but also something else, a folded piece of paper. In one swift movement, he took the tooth and the paper and quickly left the room not quite as stealthily as he had arrived.

Millie giggled as she let him into the bedroom and closed the door.

"Well done!" She kissed Joe's cheek. "She's going to be so happy tomorrow. Do you think fifty pence is enough?"

"We were lucky to get tuppence when we were kids!" Joe handed the tooth to Millie. She was about to put it in her dresser drawer when she noticed the piece of paper in his hand.

"What's that?"

"I found it under Leah's pillow; it's probably a note to the Tooth Fairy." Joe laughed softly and unfolded the paper. His laughed abruptly ended and he felt his heart drop to his feet. "You'll never believe this." Joe's hands trembled as he turned the paper and held it up for Millie to see. The gaunt face of the little boy stared out from the paper and in the soft light from their bedside lamp Millie could swear the child was laughing at her.

18

"I'm going now, but I'll be back about noon." Millie kissed Leah's forehead and grabbed her bag. "Be good for daddy."

"I will mummy." Leah said goodbye to her mum and watched as she left the kitchen. Through the closed door she heard her friend Jayne shout "hello Mrs Holden". The door opened and in rushed Jayne. "Hello Leah. I brought you an ice lolly." Jayne reached out and handed a packet to Leah who gratefully took it and ripped it open.

"Can we watch TV in your front room?" Jayne asked, her mouth full of orange flavoured ice.

Leah threw her wrapper in the cold fireplace and licked the cold raspberry flavoured lolly which had already begun to melt. "Yes, that should be OK. Mummy said not to go upstairs while daddy's outside though."

"I didn't see him out there. Where is he?" Jayne stood on her tiptoes by the kitchen sink and strained to look out of the window. "Oh there he is." She pointed and Leah jumped and looked but she couldn't quite see. Her friend was an inch or so taller than she was, which allowed her to see over the windowsill into the garden beyond.

"Come on Leah, let's watch cartoons!" Jayne bit down on her ice lolly and went through into the front room. Leah trailed behind licking the drips which had started to run down her fingers.

After half an hour of watching TV, Jayne was bored. She was sitting on the carpet stroking Moses who was lying on his back purring contentedly. Leah was sitting beside her on the floor, her fingers were sticky from her ice lolly and a line of red juice circled her mouth. Her pretty pink sun dress was liberally splattered with red dots.

Joe came in and walked to the kitchen sink to wash his hands. He'd been weeding in the vegetable garden and he was filthy and sweaty from the warm sun. He splashed the cool water on his face and rubbed some round the back of his neck. He grabbed the towel and as he dried off her realised he could hear the TV in the living room. He walked over and looked inside.

Moses spotted Joe and immediately ran to him and began nuzzling his legs, his tried and tested way of letting his human know it was time to be fed.

Jayne looked up and smiled. "Hello Mr Holden."

"Hello Jayne." Moses let out a huge howl, Joe looked down and Moses began purring again and then head-butted his leg. "I suppose you want feeding!" Leah watched as Joe gently picked up Moses and swung him onto his shoulder. Joe caught one look at Leah's face and started to laugh. "My girl, you need to wash your face! Go on, bathroom with you and get clean."

"Can we play in my room? Mummy said we could when you were back inside."

"Go on then. But make sure you wash your face and hands first." Joe smiled as the girls walked past him to go to the stairs, then his voice turned more serious. "And don't go in our room."

"Yes daddy." Leah and Jayne made a dash for the door and ran upstairs.

***

12.40pm

Jayne was lying face down on Leah's bed, a colouring book in front of her and next to it a pile of coloured wax crayons. She had spent ten minutes colouring in the picture of a teddy bear wearing a blue raincoat and yellow hat. The bear was holding a brightly coloured umbrella and was happily splashing in a puddle which covered the bottom half of his red Wellington boots.

Jayne finished the picture and closed the book. She sat up and watched as Leah carefully removed her doll's sailor dress and replace it with a ball gown. They'd been up here for ages and Jayne was bored again. Leah started brushing her doll's hair, a contented smile on her face.

"Why don't your parents let you go in their room?" Jayne asked. "I can go in my parents' room."

Leah looked over and shrugged. "I don't know. It's..." She struggled to remember the word her mum had used. "Pri-vate."

"Can we just look in there, through the door? It's already open and we aren't going to touch anything." Jayne sat on the edge of the bed. "Come on, just a quick look. No one will know!"

"I don't know that we should." Leah didn't want to get in trouble.

"Oh go on, just a quick look."

Jayne's excitement was infectious and in no time the two girls were in the hallway peeking through the open door of Millie and Joe's bedroom. Plucking up courage from her friend, Leah pushed the door open wider and stepped into the room.

The furniture inside had been changed around recently with the bed now behind the door. A chest of drawers stood in the alcove by the window and in the opposite alcove sat a large double wardrobe, with its back along the wall adjoining Leah's room. A long ottoman sat under the window which was filled with freshly laundered blankets, sheets and pillow cases.

In the corner of the room, on Millie's side of the bed was a small chest of drawers that she used as a makeshift dressing table. Behind the drawers a large mirror had been fixed to the wall, which was covered with a red chiffon scarf. On the top of the drawers sat a green glass dressing table set that had once belonged to Joe's grandmother: the covered dish filled with Millie's earrings and the candlestick barely visible from all the bangles and bracelets which currently encircled it. Millie's limited supply of make up was gathered together on a pretty china plate on the left side of the dresser with an ornate vintage hairbrush and matching hand mirror on the right.

Jayne brushed past Leah and tiptoed into the room, her eyes quickly scanned everything in case she had to make a hasty exit. Then she caught sight of Millie's jewellery and forgetting the need for secrecy she made an excited "wooo" sound and ran to the chest of drawers, her love of shiny things drawing her closer. She had just lifted the lid on the pot of earrings when Leah's voice called out: "Please don't touch, mummy will be mad."

Leah ran over to her and took the lid from Jayne and carefully sat it back down. "I wasn't going to take any out, I just wanted to..." Her voice trailed off. Leah looked at Jayne, but Jayne didn't notice as she was staring at the bed, her blue eyes huge in her slender face. Jayne's mouth opened and let out a frightened wail that seemed to come from the depths of her soul.

***

Millie was loaded down with bags and had just barely managed to open the back door and set them down. She'd met her mother in the café as usual and they had spent a pleasant hour walking round the market. Ruby had bought herself a pretty pale blue blouse which she knew would match her eyes. Millie had been able to stock up on fresh fruit and vegetables which she was going to prepare and freeze, just as soon as she'd had a cup of tea and rested her feet.

"Hello my love." Joe came into the kitchen with Moses trailing behind him. "Need help unpacking?"

"No thanks. I'll do it in a little while. Be a pal and make me a cup of tea would you, while I sort myself out." She smiled and fluttered her lashes playfully. Millie blew him a kiss and went through to the hall to hang up her coat and bag.

Millie hung her bag on its hook and had started to unbutton her coat when a terrified scream from upstairs startled her. She began to run up the starts when Jayne came racing down them, her little feet moving so fast she barely seemed to be touching the steps. Leah flew around the corner at the top of the stairs as Jayne threw herself into Millie arms and started to cry.

Millie watched in horror as Leah's foot buckled underneath her and she lurched forward, but miraculously didn't fall. Then Millie saw why... Something had a hold of Leah's dress. The material was bunched up just behind Leah's right hip as though it was being held in a fist. All Leah's weight was balanced precariously on one foot and if not for the invisible force holding her, Leah would have fallen to the bottom of the stairs. Millie couldn't bear to think of what might of happened had that been the case.

Joe had heard the scream and arrived to find Millie gently unhooking Jayne's arms from around her neck. He looked up the stairs and saw Leah teetering on the top step. "Oh my god," he whispered.

"Take her." Millie passed Jayne to him and began to climb the stairs to reach their daughter.

Leah was crying and frantically clawing at the air, trying to regain her balance. It took Millie no time to reach her and as soon as she was within touching distance, Leah's dress dropped back down to her side and she fell into her mother's arms. Millie was braced for her weight and held her tightly as she turned and ran back down the stairs.

"Millie what the hell just happened?" Joe asked Millie as she dashed past him into the living room. Millie shook her head and whispered. "I don't know."

Millie carried Leah through to the living room and sat her on the sofa; Joe followed and put Jayne down next to her. He turned away and tried to process what had just happened, but he couldn't understand why Leah didn't fall. She was leaning forward on the stairs, all her weight on one tiny foot and she didn't fall.

Jayne was still crying and wiping her eyes. She was terrified by what she had just seen and just as terrified that she would be in trouble with Leah's parents. "I'm sorry Mrs Holden. I asked to see your bedroom and Leah said we shouldn't go in there."

Millie crouched in front of the sofa. "Girls, you're not in trouble. We're not angry with you. Dry your eyes and tell me what happened."

"I saw a skellington on your bed. It had greasy black hair and no eyes. I screamed and ran away."

Joe was still trying to work out what had stopped Leah from breaking her neck in a serious fall, but Jayne's voice cut through his thoughts like a hot knife through butter. He span round and looked down at her. "What? You saw a skeleton in our room?"

Jayne nodded and wiped her eyes with the back of her hand. "It was pointing at me and laughing. I won't go in your room again I promise."

"It's alright pet, you're not in trouble. Let's get you home, I need to speak to your mum." Millie stood and took Jayne's hand. As she passed Joe she grabbed his arm, he could feel her hand shaking.

19

Saturday September 26th 1981
7pm

The living room was a shambles. The sofa was positioned under the window and was piled high with sheets, pillows and a selection of clothes belonging to Millie, Joe and Leah. The TV had been shoved back against the wall and the chair that used to sit by the window was now upstairs in Leah's bedroom. In the large space in the middle of the floor lay the double mattress from Joe and Millie's bed along side Leah's smaller mattress.

After Millie had returned from the Pember's house she heard Leah and Joe in a talking about what had happened earlier. Millie stood by the semi closed living room door and listened as Leah said she didn't see anything, she had been startled by Jayne's loud scream and had followed when she ran from the room. Joe then asked about what happened on the stairs, to which Leah replied that she'd tripped and thought her dress had caught on the banister and that is why she didn't fall.

Millie thought back to that time and felt the panic rising again. She had definitely seen something holding Leah's dress, keeping her rock steady until she had reached her. The whole thing had happened in less than four seconds: one to grab Jayne as she flung herself into her arms; the second to pass her to Joe; the third and fourth to reach Leah and pluck her to safety. But while it was happening it seemed as though it was all in slow motion, the time dragging until Leah was safely in her arms.

When Millie had taken Jayne home, the child had promptly burst into tears again at the sight of her mother. Linda listened patiently as Jayne told her through rasping sobs what she had seen in Millie's bedroom. It took several minutes and the promise of a few treats to calm Jayne, but eventually the tears subsided and her bright smile returned. After Jayne was settled in the living room in front of the TV with some ice cream, Millie took Linda in to the kitchen and told her what she had witnessed on the stairs. She began to shake uncontrollably as the shock finally set in so Linda offered her a brandy 'for medicinal purposes'.

Three glasses later, Millie felt better and was ready to go back home and talk with Joe. Leah's safety was paramount in her mind and Millie didn't feel she could keep her safe in this house. Not only was the place haunted by some devil's spawn, but Jellyman next door had proven to be trouble as well. This was not a house for children. Whether Joe liked it or not they had to leave. Prepared for battle, Millie opened the living room door and walked into the room.

"Millie, are you OK?" Joe saw her sway slightly as she entered.

"Me? Yes, I'm fine, just a tit bipsy!" Millie kicked off her shoes and tiptoed to the sofa, then sat down heavily in the seat nearest the kitchen door. Leah giggled and scooted over to sit beside her mother. Millie wrapped her arms around her and kissed the top of her head. "What have you been up to my loves?"

"Millie, Leah and I have been talking and she tells me she's a bit scared of going upstairs, isn't that right Shortie?" Leah nodded shyly. "So, I thought that we should all sleep down here for the time being. How do you feel about camping out in the living room for a few nights?" Joe had been sitting in the chair by the window, but he got up and came to sit beside Leah on the sofa.

"What do you think mummy?" Leah looked up and gazed at Millie, her eyes huge in her tiny face.

Millie thought for a few seconds and the idea actually began to appeal to her, but only as a short term solution. "I think it's an excellent idea. It will be a lot of work though."

"Yeah for me, you're too drunk to stand!" Joe laughed and Leah giggled. Millie reached over and play swatted him on the leg. "Ouch!" Leah laughed harder, enjoying the banter between her parents.

"Right you wimp, if you want to sleep down here, we have to get to work!" Millie announced and so began three hours of work.

Leah was told to stay in the kitchen and keep out of the way while mummy and daddy were busy. In that time they had cleared the furniture out the way and brought down the mattresses from their beds. Joe was busy making sandwiches in the kitchen while Leah was helping Millie to put sheets on the makeshift beds.

Millie was sitting cross legged in the centre of her mattress putting clean cases on the pillows. She looked at Leah who was busy spreading a blanket on her bed. "Are you happy here? In this house I mean."

Leah tucked in the bottom edge of the blanket and sat down. She thought for a long time then slowly shook her head. "No mummy, it's scary here and I don't want to go outside because the old man scares me. I don't like it."

Millie reached over and stroked her face. "I'm sorry." Leah looked at her with sad eyes and whispered: "it's OK."

"No, it's not OK. Your happiness is important to me and your daddy. How would you feel if we found a new house to move into, one without a creepy old man next door so you can play in the garden?"

Leah smiled, but then her face dropped. "But... What about Jayne? I won't be able to see her every day."

"You will see her every day at school and in the holidays you can visit each other. There are sandwiches on the kitchen table; best get them before Moses does!" Joe said from the doorway.

"Thank you daddy!" Leah was starving and she wasted no time in getting up and dashing into the kitchen.

Millie got up and went to Joe. He pulled her close as soon as she was in touching distance. "Millie, I'm sorry. For all those times you told me you thought we should leave and I wouldn't listen. It should not have taken seeing our daughter in danger to agree to move house."

"None of that would have happened if I hadn't insisted on leaving 41. All the crap we've gone through... it's my fault... I insisted on us coming here!" Millie buried her face in Joe's chest.

Joe placed his hands on either side of Millie's face and tilted it upwards so their eyes met. "You are not to blame. You weren't to know what was going to happen once we set foot inside the door. You said something similar when Jayne got injured, remember?" Millie nodded.

"I told you then and I'll tell you again, it was not your fault. At any time I could have put my foot down and refused to move, but I didn't I understood why you needed to leave that old house and I still do. There is no fault and if there is, then I share some of that with you." Joe kissed her hard on the lips and stared into her eyes. "I love you Mrs!"

"I love you too sweetheart." Millie pulled Joe's head back down for one more kiss which was rudely interrupted by her stomach growling ferociously. "Did you mention food? I'm starving!"

20

Monday September 28th 1981
12.40pm

"Can I speak to Rob please?" Millie asked the young blonde girl, whose name she could never remember.

"I'm afraid Mr Mickelwright is out for lunch and will be in meetings all afternoon." Came the bored reply, the lady didn't even raise her head to look at Millie.

Millie was tired and in no mood to be messed with, she'd seen Rob's car in the car park on her way into the building so she knew he was here somewhere. Millie quickly looked behind her and saw the top of Rob's head through his office window.

"Out is he? I suppose that's a mirage then!" The young girl looked up just in time to see Millie marching to Rob's office door.

"Oi! You can't go in there?" The young lady screeched from behind her desk.

"Watch me!" Millie called over her shoulder as she rapped sharply on the glass.

Rob was just finishing his tuna sandwich when he heard the commotion outside in the entrance hall. He drained the last of his tea to wash down the bread and bits of fish still clinging stubbornly to his teeth. He was about to leave when Millie knocked on his office door and entered the room.

Millie's pretty face was pale and she had dark circles around her usually bright blue eyes. "Millie, what the hell's the matter?" Rob came out of his seat and quickly grabbed a chair for her to sit in. She gratefully took it and sat down with a sigh.

"Rob, I hate to ask, but what are the chances of us being able to move house?"

Rob went back to his seat and dropped down into it with a bump. "You can't be serious, you only just moved in!"

"I'm deadly serious. The place is unsuitable for us and Leah is finding it difficult to settle there."

"What's going on Millie? You look terrible..." Rob smiled at her sour look. "Sorry, but you've definitely looked better wench!"

"Thanks Rob, I know I look a mess. I slept like crap because my daughter is too scared to go upstairs so we are all sleeping in the living room."

"Kids are always afraid of monsters under the bed Millie, that's no reason to sleep down stairs! That doesn't make much sense."

"The house is haunted..." Rob's laughter cut her off.

"Go on laugh all you like, but I'm deadly serious." Rob had known Millie for a good many years and had always respected her for her frankness and honesty. He looked at the determined expression on her face and knew she was telling him the truth as she saw it.

"We've had things go missing that turned up elsewhere and we hear footsteps and bangs through out the whole house. My brother's girlfriend had something run its hands all over her a few months back and she's not been back since, not that I blame her. Oh and there's the ghost of a young kid upstairs that loves to piss off the neighbour next door. Did you know the old bastard reported us to social services because he thought the ghost upstairs was our daughter and we were neglecting her?"

"I did hear on the grapevine that someone had made a prank call about you. But I knew it was bollocks so I didn't ask too much about it."

"That ghost kid decided to frighten our neighbour's girl a couple of days ago. She ran down our stairs screaming and now my daughter is too scared to even go to the bathroom by herself. And because of that filthy pig next door, she's too scared to go outside and play. We have to get out Rob!"

He leaned forward in his seat and clasped his hands together on the table. "Millie, I really am sorry, but we have nothing we can offer you. I would dearly love to help but there's nothing free at the moment."

"Not even a two bedroom house?"

Rob watched as Millie sank dejectedly in the chair. "Not even a two bedroom flat."

"Well, that's that then!" Millie tiredly stood up. "I won't take up any more of your time. Thanks for seeing me Rob."

"You didn't give me much choice." Rob smiled at Millie and got up to open the door for her.

Outside in the entrance hall the young blonde receptionist was taking the particulars of an elderly lady. She slyly looked up as Millie and Rob came out of his office. "We'll put that on the board for you right away Mrs Horobin. Best of luck." She smiled as the old lady thanked her and then watched disinterested as she slowly walked away from the desk.

"Thanks again Rob. If anything does come available please let me know."

"I will Millie. Now go home and get some sleep." He patted her back and left to go back into his office.

"Millie Holden is that you?" Millie turned to see a small grey haired old lady behind her.

"Yes... Sheila?" Millie hugged the old lady and stepped back. "How are you? I've not seen you in years!"

"Not since we were neighbours in Talbot House! I'm still there in the same flat and our Gail's still with me."

"Isn't she courting yet?"

"No love, too busy studying to be a nurse for all that malarkey. Our Martin is living with us now an' all since his Mrs kicked him out. Poor thing has to sleep on the sofa, what with my little place only having two bedrooms."

"That's a shame. He works at the same factory as me. We're always bumping into each other, but he never let on that his marriage was in trouble. How is he?"

"He's alright, better away from all the shouting if you ask me. He really can't stay on the sofa forever, but he doesn't want to move out. He says it's because he likes my cooking too much." The old lady's face crinkled around the eyes as she smiled. "He's a good lad so I don't mind him staying with us but that flat is too small for all of us, so I'm looking for an exchange. There's bound to be someone out there living on their own in a big house who wouldn't mind swapping it for a flat."

Millie burst into laughter and hugged the old lady. "Oh what's that for?"

"Sheila, you are my fairy godmother and I love you. Now, how about I buy you a cup of tea and you let me tell you about the lovely big house we live in."

***

3.35pm

"I'm getting to that Joe, give me chance. Well, Sheila's still living in Talbot House and her kids are living with her, you remember Gail and Martin?" Joe nodded and waved his hand at her, hoping she would get to the point of her tale. "Well, both of her kids want to stay with her. Martin's going through a messy divorce and Gail never left home so Sheila's looking for someone who might want to exchange a three bedroom house with her lovely little two bedroom flat. So...." Millie sipped at her tea and sheepishly looked at Joe over the top of her mug.

Joe sat opposite Millie at the kitchen table, his empty mug sitting in front of him. He tried to look stern, but his mouth curved slightly at the corners as he fought back a smile. He waited for her to continue but when she just sat there daintily drinking her tea he let out an exasperated: "So....?"

"So..... I told her about us wanting to move and that we're looking for something smaller and I asked if she would consider our place." Again Millie stopped to drink from her mug.

"So what did Sheila say?"

"She's...."

"Millie please, for love of god, just tell me!"

"Oh you're no fun!" Millie pouted. Joe growled low in his throat and started to get out of his seat. Millie put a hand up and chuckled, "she's coming over this weekend to have a look at the place."

Joe sat back in his chair and smiled at Millie. "Really?" Millie nodded and smiled back. "You didn't tell her about any of the crap that goes on here did you?"

"No way, I didn't want to put her off."

Joe leaned back in his chair and rubbed his hands over his face. He dropped them in to his lap and looked at Millie. "I never ever thought I'd say this but I can't wait to be out of this bloody place. It can go to the bloody devil!"

No sooner had Joe finished speaking his mug flew across the room and smashed against the fire place. Millie screamed and jumped out of her seat and watched in horror as the kitchen cupboards opened and closed by themselves. The lights in the kitchen blinked on and off repeatedly and the TV in the living room turned on, the volume rising to a deafening level.

In the kitchen of the adjoining house, Victor was sitting in his filthy leather chair dozing in front of the fire. His head was tipped back and rested against the heavily stained chair back, but occasionally it rolled forward and jolted him awake. He wasn't comfortable but was too tired to climb the stairs to his own bed. The crash of something heavy hitting the fire place startled him, then the sounds of banging and somebody screeching like a banshee echoed through the wall.

Victor struggled to get to his feet and by the time he'd managed to stand, he could hear the TV next door blasting. He reached for his sturdy iron poker and thumped heavily on the kitchen wall. "NOISY BASTARDS! KEEP THE FUCKING RACKET DOWN!"

Joe ran into the living room and yanked the TV plug out the wall instantly cutting off its noise. He walked back into the kitchen and heard Jellyman shouting and banging the wall. The cupboards doors had stopped their frantic movements and the lights had stopped flickering. He looked for Millie but she was no where to be found and the kitchen door was ajar. Packets and tins lay everywhere as though a spoiled child had wilfully thrown them around the room. A tin of tomato soup fell from the cupboard and landed on the ground with a loud thud.

Moses hissed and bolted towards the open door. "No Moses!" Joe called out and frantically grabbed the cat just as he was about to escape outside. He cradled Moses in his arms like a baby and walked outside to look for Millie. He found her standing by her vegetable garden. "Are you OK love?" She nodded in reply but didn't face him.

"Leah will be home from school soon, I'll go and clean up the kitchen. I don't want her to see the mess and then have to explain what happened. Are you coming in?"

"Just give me a few minutes." Millie turned and stroked Joe's arm, then tickled Moses' ear.

"OK love." Joe leaned forward and kissed Millie's forehead. Moses wriggled in Joe's arms and meowed in protest at being crushed between the two humans.

21

"Only a week to go Millie. Are you excited?" Frank slowed to a stop at the top of Coventry Road and flicked the left indicator.

"You're joking right? I can't bloody wait. Are you sure you'll be able to borrow Dave's van?" Millie asked, braced her hands on the dashboard as Frank quickly pulled the car to a stop behind a bus collecting new passengers. He waited for a break in traffic so he could manoeuvre around the bus and as soon as the last car had passed he pulled out and continued down the street.

"Yeah, no worries. I'll let him know tonight when you want it for and I can pick it up the night before and drop it back on the evening when we're done. As long as we replace the fuel he's happy." Frank slowed the car for the right turn in to New Street. "Did they like the place?"

"They loved it and the garden, Sheila's already got plans for a pond and a lawn." Millie waved to Martha Brookes as the car passed her by, she didn't wave back. Millie tutted then remembered why she was sitting in Frank's car. "By the way, thanks for picking me up today. I couldn't have managed to carry all these boxes back to the house."

"No bother pet. Do you want me to ask Yvonne to save you some from the supermarket?"

"That would be great thanks." Frank turned into Baggott's Circle and Millie dug in her bag for her house keys. "I'm so glad you're back together, she's a lovely girl."

Frank smiled and let out a long sigh, "yeah, she is."

Millie glanced up at her brother and saw the flush on his cheeks. "Are you blushing?" She laughed and poked his cheek with her finger. "You are, you're blushing. Oh god this is beautiful!"

"Leave off Millie!" Frank pulled the car to and abrupt stop outside Millie's house making her jolt forward in her seat. She was about to swear when she heard her name being shouted. Millie looked out the window and saw Linda running towards the car.

"Millie, you best hurry, he's going berserk!" Linda yanked the car door open before Millie had chance to grab the handle.

Millie got out the car with a confused look on her face. A short distance away she could hear banging and Jellyman's distinctive voice echoed from the vicinity of her back door. "What's going on?"

"Your neighbour is in your back garden thumping your back door and yelling at the top of his voice. I got back from fetching the girls from school about fifteen minutes ago and it was all quiet. Five minutes later I hear your neighbour making all sorts of noise in your back garden.

The loud banging continued then Jellyman screeched "COME OUT HERE YOU LITTLE SHIT, I KNOW YOU'RE IN THERE!"

Millie was angry beyond reason and had started running before he was halfway through his sentence. She reached the gate and opened it with a forceful shove. Jellyman was still hammering on the door with a clenched fist and calling out to someone inside the house. Millie started to approach him but the stench he gave off made her gag and step back.

"What the fuck do you think you're doing you mad old bastard?" Millie's voice startled Victor. He stopped and turned to face her, his arm still raised to strike the door. Millie's cheeks were bright red with emotion and her barely controlled anger made her voice shake. Frank appeared behind her and put his hand on her shoulder to try and calm her down but she shrugged it off and pointed an accusing finger in Jellyman's direction.

Victor was a man who was not easily intimidated, but this crazy woman standing less than two feet away scared him half to death. His own anger returned as he recalled what had brought him here.

He had been feeding and exercising his birds as he always did in the afternoon and as usual the scrawny kid next door had been watching him. It was almost an everyday occurrence and over time he had become immune to the stares and the laughter, but today it had rubbed him the wrong way.

Victor's favourite bird had died during the night and he was unusually saddened by this. He'd taken the bird and buried at the bottom of his garden. As he was walking back towards his shed a movement in the upstairs window caught his eye and again he saw the brat staring at him. However, this time she was mocking him, pretending to cry and wiping away fake tears from her dark soulless eyes.

He had been infuriated by the heartless bitch's actions and he wasted no time in returning to the bottom of the garden and squeezing through the gap in the hedge. He'd marched purposefully down the garden all the while looking at the window and every time he looked up he saw the kid pointing at him and making faces at him.

When he reached the vegetable patch he stopped to get his breath and looked up at the window. The kid was still pointing and making angry faces at him. Victor hated that kid and standing as straight as his widow's stoop would allow, he shook his fist at the window and yelled: "I hate you, you disrespectful little bastard. I hope you rot in hell!"

The child in the window snarled down at him, her face contorting and twisting as she silently growled out her frustration through the closed window. Her eyebrows were drawn together over her dark eyes which glared down angrily at him. Undeterred Victor walked to the back door and banged on the glass for all he was worth, all the time yelling for the kid to face him.

He looked again at Millie who was still standing and pointing at him. "Answer me! What gives you the right to trespass in our back yard?"

"I want to see that kid of yours an' teach her some fucking manners! You need to teach her some respect, every day the nosey shit stares at me and I've had it up to here!" He held his hand up to his forehead.

"You truly are losing your mind. There's no one in there. My husband is working late and my daughter has been at school all day." Millie stopped and cleared her throat. "You won't believe me, but you're seeing the 'ghost kid' that is always haunts upstairs." Millie hadn't planned on telling him about the ghost, but now she was glad she had, the look on his face was priceless.

Victor sneered at her. "You're making it up to get that brat of yours out of trouble. I know what I saw and it was her!" Millie shook her head and was about to ask Linda to tell him that she had collected Leah from school, but a little voice interrupted.

"Mummy what's the matter?" Leah's face peeked around from behind her mother's side. Auntie Linda had told her to stay indoors while she went out to speak to her mother. But after a couple of minutes, Leah heard her mother shouting and she wanted to make sure she was OK, so she left the house and saw the crowd gathered by her family's back gate.

Victor looked down and he felt like he'd been punched in the gut. She kind of looked similar to the face he had been seeing in the upstairs window, but the bone structure was all wrong. They both had the same dark hair but where the kid upstairs had a thin pasty face, this girl had round cheeks and glowing skin from playing out in the sun. Slowly he came to the realisation that what the mouthy wench had told him might have been true. That this couldn't have been the child he saw upstairs.

Frank saw the look on the old man's face and pulled Millie out the way. He came towards the old man and his smell caught him off guard. Frank coughed to clear his throat and motioned the old man forward towards the open gate. "Listen mate, you don't look too well. If I were you I'd go home and get myself a cup of tea."

Victor looked up and blinked at the dark haired young man beside him who was smiling at him. He nodded his head, a cup of tea sounded good about now. He licked his lips and began to slowly walk up the path towards the

112

street. Frank followed behind Victor as he walked back to his own house, chatting merrily to him about any old thing.

Millie shook her head as she watched the two walk away, grateful to Frank for helping get rid of the insane old git from next door.

"Will you be OK Mill?" Linda pulled Millie into her arms and gave her a comforting hug.

Millie nodded and returned the hug. "You're an angel you know. I'm going to miss you when we go. You will visit won't you?"

"Try and keep me away." Linda pulled away and kissed her cheek, then reached over to stroke Leah's head. "Look after your mum OK!"

Leah nodded and watched as Linda walked back home quickly wiping her eyes as she went.

***

Victor pushed the door shut behind him and leant against it for support. He couldn't understand what had happened. He had to have seen their kid in the window, it had to be her! The wench next door said it was a ghost, but there was no way it was. Ghosts didn't exist, but how else could he explain the child in the upstairs window when there was no one home.

The day after he'd called social services to report the kid being left home alone, he'd had a phone call telling him that they would not be following up the case. The lady he had spoken to was quite put out to have visited the place and found nothing untoward. She had accused him of making a false claim and reminded him that wasting their time could result in prosecution. He had insisted he'd seen the child but the silly cow wouldn't listen. Now he knew it wasn't their child he'd seen, but who the hell was it? Maybe the wench next door was telling the truth.

"No. No. NO! Ghosts don't exist. It had to have been her I saw!" He pushed away from the door and started to walk through to the kitchen when a noise on the stairs stopped him in his tracks. He couldn't see anything amiss among the newspapers and other detritus that covered each step. Victor shook his head and began to walk through the living room door but was halted by another noise that sounded like the fluttering of wings.

He took a step back and flicked the light switch. The light came on and illuminated the staircase, but there was nothing there. Then, as he was about to turn off the light, he heard it again: the sound of something skittering around on the landing at the top of the stairs and also, the flapping of wings.

Victor took hold of the banister and began to climb the stairs, one step at a time. He had reached the fourth step when he was caught off guard by the noise which seemed to emanate from the landing. He looked up and saw the grey body and pearlescent green head of a pigeon.

"What the bloody hell are you doing there?" The bird cooed and walked towards the edge of the top step. Victor couldn't believe what he was looking at. He never left any of his windows open and couldn't explain how the bird had got into the house. He continued his slow climb up the stairs and by the time he had reached the ninth step, he was startled again by the noise, but this time it was much louder. He swayed slightly on the step and in an effort to keep his balance he gripped the banister with both hands and held on tightly. He looked up to the landing as he heard more flapping of wings and saw four more pigeons flutter down to the floor.

He was anxious that his birds had found a way into his home and that he might not be able to get them to the safety of the shed. Victor quickened his pace and as he finally put his foot on the top step a flock of at least thirty birds erupted from the bathroom and flew towards him. He threw his arms up to protect his face and immediately lost his balance.

The world slipped from underneath him as he fell backwards into the void, the noise from the birds drowned out by the blood curdling scream as he bounced hard on the stairs. Victor cried out in pain as he landed heavily on his curved spine, he heard the 'crack' and knew he it had broken from the impact. His arms and legs were twisted at odd angles and his head hit the corner of the wall by the front door with a solid 'thwack' making him instantly lose consciousness.

A few moments later he woke to the sound of a child laughing. He was frightened and couldn't feel anything apart from a warm sensation at the back of his head as blood poured from the gash behind his ear. He opened his eyes, though his vision was blurred, he saw his birds had gone. He briefly closed his eyes and again he heard the sound of a child laughing. He struggled to open his eyes again but after a few seconds they finally responded and he was shocked to see a naked boy with a pale skinny body and lank shoulder length hair kneeling by his side.

The boy looked down at Victor as he lay prone on the floor, then his face broke into the same snarling glare Victor had seen in the upstairs window. Victor's eyes flared wide and a single tear rolled down his swollen face. He whimpered and tried to move away from the menacing child beside him, but his broken body refused to obey.

The boy leaned close to Victor's face and through gritted teeth he snarled: "See you in hell Old Man!"

22

Saturday October 24th 1981
12.45pm

The house was almost empty after Millie, Joe, Frank and a couple of the neighbours had spent the morning carrying boxes and furniture out to the large van parked on the road in front of 33. But they were leaving with far less than they arrived with. Since she had met Sheila Horobin almost a month ago, Millie had been sorting through all her nick-knacks and keeping only the best, or most sentimental, of items and as a result had halved all their possessions.

Leah had made a fuss when Millie started to whittle down her toy collection, but Joe had taken her aside and told her that the unwanted items would be going to the local children's hospital. He'd said: "wouldn't it be wonderful if you could help to make them feel a little bit better by letting them play with all your old toys?" Leah had thought about it and decided that she wanted to make their stay in hospital a bit brighter by letting her old toys go to them. She felt very grown up and proud of herself.

Now, after all that sorting and boxing had been done, it was moving day and Millie was desperately unhappy to be leaving. This was supposed to have been her dream home, but it had turned in to a nightmare the second they had walked through the door. As the weeks had gone on, more and more weird things had been happening, however, this last week or so, the house had been eerily quiet: there were no noises, the airing cupboard door and attic hatch stayed in place and nothing went missing.

Bizarrely even Jellyman hadn't made his presence known, which was unusual to say the least. They hadn't once heard him call his birds in, yet they were still out flying every day. Millie had thought that he was ashamed after his antics last week and was keeping a low profile, what ever he was up to she was grateful she hadn't had to deal with any more screeching from him.

Millie shuddered and grabbed the broom from by the fireplace and began to sweep the kitchen floor. She was nearly finished when her mother walked in from the living room. "Millie, the upstairs is clean. What else needs doing?"

Millie opened the kitchen door and flicked the pile of dust outside to be carried away by the cool breeze. "Just the kitchen units to be wiped through now, but I can do that." She sniffed and wiped her eyes with the back of her hand.

"Millie love, come here." Ruby stood with her arms opened wide and in the next instant Millie was in them being held tight as she cried out her frustration and sadness. "It's OK chick, don't cry."

"Oh Mum, I don't want to leave."

"I know you're sad, but you're doing the right thing. Trust me, this is for the best." Ruby stroked Millie's back.

"I know, I know..." Millie pulled back and wiped her eyes, her tears finally subsiding. "I had such hopes for this place. But right from day one the house let us know that we aren't welcome here."

Ruby gave a short laugh. "Don't you think you're being a bit melodramatic?"

Irritated by her mother's response, Mille moved away and Ruby's arms fell to her sides. "Not at all. You know of the weird shit that's happened here, it really feel's like the house, or who ever is hanging around the place, rejected us right from the start. Hopefully Sheila and her kids will be luckier than we were."

"I hope you're right chick." Ruby smiled at her daughter. "I don't tell you anywhere near enough but, I love you."

Millie felt a warm glow in her chest and she returned her mother's smile. She closed the space between them and kissed Ruby's cheek. "I love you too Mum. Now, let's get those cupboards clean."

***

2.20pm

The house sat lonely and soulless in the afternoon sun, its life seemed to have evaporated with the last box that had been loaded on to the van. The doors and windows had been opened to allow a cool breeze into the property, but it was as though the house was in a bubble and nothing could penetrate the invisible shell that enclosed it.

Joe and Millie stood side by side in the living room watching Leah through the open window as she said goodbye to Jayne. Joe checked his watch again and let out a long sigh. "They'll be here soon. I'm going to do one more walk through to make sure we've got everything."

"I'll check upstairs." Millie volunteered. Joe looked surprised but didn't argue, he knew that determined look on Millie's face all too well. He smiled and watched her walk through the living room door, her strides purposeful and defiant as though challenging the house to do something in the last few minutes they had in the place.

Joe went to the pantry first and checked the cupboards in there which took no time at all. He walked back into the kitchen and go on his hands and knees to look in the cupboard under the sink. The sound of a slamming door upstairs startled him and he jolted upwards, banging the top of his head on the underside of the sink.

Joe stood up slowly and leant against the sink unit, all the time he rubbed the sore spot on his head. He looked out the window and saw his shed, he'd miss that old thing and being able to use the garden tools it held, but he couldn't take it with him. He was leaving it here for Martin to make use of and he knew it would be in safe hands. Joe spared his shed one last look and was about to walk across the room to check the last of the cupboards when an ear piercing scream stopped him in his tracks.

***

118

Millie straightened her spine and walked through the door. She really wasn't at all as confident as her demeanour portrayed but with determined set to her jaw, she griped the banister and began the climb to the top of the stairs.

The atmosphere felt oddly different up here compared to downstairs, it was heavy and oppressive. The air felt charged, like in the moments before a lightning strike, making the hairs on Millie's arms stand on end. It felt warmer up here too, but as Millie passed the bathroom door she shivered as an icy blast of air enveloped her body. Millie stopped and rubbed her arms in an effort to warm up, but it did no good, she was chilled to the marrow and she could see her breath in front of her.

She stepped forward in the direction of Leah's old room and she had almost reached the open door when it slammed shut in her face. She pressed a hand to her chest and felt her heart pounding. Her breathing was erratic making her feel light headed. She reached up and turned the handle but the door refused to budge. Her voice barely above a whisper, she called out: "fine you little bastard, keep your door locked!"

Millie was startled by the sound of footsteps running across the ceiling. She swallowed hard and looked upwards and saw a dark void where the attic hatch should have been. She stepped away from the door and continued along the hall to the small bedroom and looking in the open doorway, she could see the room was empty. She turned to her right and took a step towards her old bedroom but as soon as she crossed the threshold a bolt of blue electricity sent her flying backwards. She landed hard against the banister, she cried out in pain as the wood bit into her hip.

Millie leant against the banister for support as she struggled to stand upright. Her legs felt shaky and it felt like they might give way any second. "OK, you win you little fucker!" She said between clenched teeth as she turned and began to walk back down the landing.

As soon as she walked under the opening to the attic, the torso of the emaciated young boy dropped in front of her, his body hanging upside down from the black space above. The boys face resembled that of a corpse with its sunken cheeks and dark eye sockets. He held his hands at the level of his head and waved them menacingly at Millie, all the while he laughed as she screamed in fright.

Millie held her hands in front of her face and bolted for the stairs. The boy's ethereal body evaporated as Millie ran through it but his high pitched laughter continued and followed her until she reached the safety of the front garden.

Epilogue

Saturday October 31st 1981

3.47pm

"He's dead?" Millie couldn't quite believe what Linda had told her. "How did you find out?"

"Thursday afternoon. I was walking down our street when I saw this woman banging on Jellyman's front door and shouting through the mail slot trying to get him to answer. When she saw me cross the road she asked if I'd seen him, but I hadn't since the day he was on your yard. When was that Mill?"

Millie sat back on the sofa and tried to count back to that day. "It was Friday... the sixteenth."

Linda nodded and continued: "His sister said that she brought shopping for him every Thursday afternoon and left it by his back gate. She said that when she bought his shopping last week, the bags she left the week before hadn't been taken in. She was frantic with worry, so I offered to call the police, just in case something had happened to him." Linda stopped and drank the rest of her tea.

Millie waited as patiently as she could, but then curiosity got the better of her. "So, what did happen to him Lin?"

"It's a bit gross actually. When the police got there they had to break down the door..."

Millie held her hand up. "Hang on, didn't she have a set of keys to get in?"

"I asked her that but she said that years ago he changed the locks and wouldn't let her have a spare set of keys. He was paranoid that she would go in there and steal his stuff. Anyway, the police broke down the door, but they couldn't open the blasted thing. As it turned out, Jellyman was lying behind it and from what I overheard; he'd been there at least ten days."

"Oh my god, the poor man!"

"Poor man, have you forgotten what he was like?" Linda was shocked that her friend could show such empathy for him.

"No, but I didn't wish him dead. Do they know how it happened?"

"They think he fell down the stairs. He was a bit of a hoarder and had newspapers stacked on the stair case, the silly sod probably tripped on some of them. Apparently the place was filthy and stunk like a sewer, how much of that was the mess and how much was caused by him lying there for nearly two weeks is anyone's guess."

Millie shuddered and got up to take her mug back into the kitchen, Linda followed behind. "This place is lovely Millie; you have such a great view." Linda crossed to the window and looked out over the fields and hedge rows which stretched out as far as the eye could see. Directly behind Talbot House was the Wyrley and Essington canal with a solitary barge making slow progress along its length.

Linda looked back at Millie and asked: "How does Leah like it?"

Millie smiled. "She loves it. She misses your Jayne of course, but she's made a couple of new friends here. How are your new neighbours?"

Linda returned Millie's smile. "Really nice people, I haven't been round there yet but I have spoken to Sheila in passing and she's a very nice lady."

"Have they... umm... had any weird stuff happen there?" Millie looked shyly at Linda.

Linda shook her curly head. "I don't think so. She's never mentioned anything about it in the few times we've spoken and I didn't like to ask." Linda started to laugh. "Can you imagine it, me asking that nice little old lady 'Oi Mrs! Has that ghost been rummaging through your drawers lately?'"

Millie joined in with Linda's laughter. It felt good to laugh and release the knot of tension she still carried away from that house. The family had been in their flat on the thirteenth floor precisely one week and since the last time she left the house, she had lived under a cloud. The face of the boy in the attic haunted her dreams and she could still hear his maniacal laughter when she was by herself.

Linda wiped the tears from her eyes and looked over at Millie who was holding her stomach and still giggling like a school girl. "I should get going cherub, it's been lovely catching up with you again."

Millie crossed the short distance to her friend and threw her arms around her shoulders. "I love you matey! Send our love to everyone and tell Joan to pay us a visit soon."

"I will." Linda hugged her friend then went back into the living room to put on her coat which was draped over the arm of the sofa. As she was busy fastening the buttons a thought occurred to her. "Oh, you know, there was something else strange about Jellyman. When they finally moved him, they found a load of pigeon feathers lying underneath his body and no one knows how they got there."

Millie picked up Linda's bag and passed it to her. "That's odd. Now you mention it, that last week we were there we saw his birds flying but didn't hear him outside calling them back in. What's going to happen to them?"

Linda walked down the long hallway, Millie trailing on her heals. When they reached the door Linda said: "By all accounts they've 'flown the coop' as it were. They must have been hungry and went off looking for food and never came back."

Millie opened the door and held it for Linda to go through. As she walked past, she kissed Millie on the cheek. "Look after yourself Mill, give my love to Joe and Leah. I'll see you soon."

"Bye Lin, take care!" Millie watched as Linda walked down the corridor to the lift and pressed the button. After a few seconds the lift made a 'ping' noise and the doors opened. The friends blew quick kisses to each other and Linda disappeared from sight.

Millie closed the door and locked it then made her way through to the kitchen. She couldn't help feeling sorry for old Jellyman, no one deserved to die like that. To fall and lie undiscovered for two weeks, how frightened and lonely he must have been.

Millie busied herself with washing the mugs and wiping the counter in the kitchen, her thoughts straying to 33 Baggott's Circle and its new residents. She mused aloud: "Wouldn't it be ironic if the Horobins didn't experience any of the strange things we did? Well at least that evil little shit didn't follow us here!"

Just then a tapping on the kitchen window drew Millie's attention. She turned and saw a solitary pigeon perched there, cooing softly and pecking the glass with its tiny beak. She walked over and shooed it away by waving her cloth at it. The bird launched itself and flew away as quickly as it had arrived.

Millie started to walk back towards the sink when she heard more tapping at the window. She looked back to see four more pigeons sitting there, each of them vying for space on the narrow window ledge. Again she waved her cloth, but this time she ran to the window, in a sudden burst of flight the birds dispersed.

Millie went back to the sink and began to rinse her cloth under the hot tap. She finished and shut off the water and became aware of loud tapping noise, but this time it was coming from the living room. She crept to the kitchen door and peered through into the other room, staring in disbelief she saw a crowd of grey pigeons huddled together on the ledge of the large window that ran the width of the living room.

The birds cooed and pecked each other, some jumped and flew away when larger birds demanded ownership of their space, but all of them appeared to be looking inside the window at Millie as she warily approached.

She could still hear the tapping on the windowpane and tried to pinpoint which bird was making the noise, but there must have been twenty pigeons on the ledge and finding the culprit was going to be difficult.

Then, as she looked at the group she saw a tiny hand, the fingers pale and skeletal, reaching through the throng of birds to tap the window with its chipped and dirty fingernails. Millie drew nearer to the window, not quite believing what she was seeing, when suddenly the hand balled into a fist and slammed against the window. Millie screamed and dropped to her knees in fright, using her hands to shield her head in case the glass shattered. After a few seconds, she uncurled herself and stealthily crawled to the window and peeked through the glass. The birds had disappeared and so had the bony hand, all that remained was a solitary grey feather which floated on the breeze to land on the window ledge.

Printed in Great Britain
by Amazon